Mermaid Magic

Gwyneth Rees is half Welsh and half English and was brought up in Scotland. She went to Glasgow University and qualified as a doctor in 1990. She is a child and adolescent psychiatrist and has worked in several places, including Birmingham and London. She now works part-time in order to write and is the author of the fabulous *Fairy Dust* and, for older readers, the warm and moving *The Mum Hunt*. She lives in London with her two cats.

3 books in 1

Mermaid Magic

Gwyneth Rees

Illustrated by Annabel Hudson

MACMILLAN CHILDREN'S BOOKS

Mermaid Magic, *Rani's Sea Spell* and *The Shell Princess* first published 2001
by Macmillan Children's Books

This edition first published 2003 by Macmillan Children's Books
a division of Macmillan Publishers Limited
20 New Wharf Road, London N1 9RR
Basingstoke and Oxford
www.panmacmillan.com

Associated companies throughout the world

ISBN 0 330 42632 X

3 5 7 9 8 6 4 2

A CIP catalogue record for this book is available from
the British Library

Typeset by SX Composing DTP, Rayleigh, Essex
Printed and bound in Great Britain by Mackays of Chatham plc, Kent

Mermaids

Mermaid
Magic

For Mum and Dad, with love

Chapter one

Rani swam down through the turquoise water until her belly was flat against the sandy bottom of the seabed. Then she did a quick flip with her tail so that she somersaulted upwards again.

"*Show-off!*" she heard, as she flicked her hair out of her eyes.

She looked suspiciously at her pet sea horse, Roscoe, who had been perched on a nearby rock with his mouth shut the whole time, looking innocently in her direction. Strange things had been happening to Rani recently. She kept hearing odd, whispery words when nobody near her had spoken. At first she had thought it was just Roscoe playing tricks on her but the little sea horse had denied it.

Before she could give it any more thought, the conch sounded. That meant it was time for them to go back into the school cave for more lessons. Rani swam over to where her sister, Kai, was sitting on a rock twisting her long blonde hair into a tight spiral. Rani hadn't told Kai about the strange whispers. For some reason she felt that she should keep them secret. Which was strange because she and Kai always told each other everything.

"School is boring, boring, boring," complained Kai loudly, letting go of her hair so that it swished out into a gold mass that enveloped her. She flicked herself off the rock and kicked up a load of sand with her tail, nearly bumping into Marissa and Marina, the twins, who swished their golden tresses outwards proudly as they swam by.

Rani sighed. She wished she had beautiful golden hair like all the other mermaids. Her mother kept telling her that her red hair was beautiful too, but Rani didn't think so.

The conch sounded again just as a whole shoal of rainbow fish swam past, heading towards the reef at top speed.

"What's the hurry?" Kai called out after them.

"Our babies are hatching!" one of the fish called back.

"Wow!" exclaimed Kai. "I've never seen baby fish hatching before. Let's go and see!"

And before Rani had time to protest that they really should go back to school,

Kai had set off after the fish.

"I suppose we could always say we didn't hear the conch," Rani muttered doubtfully, as she followed her sister.

Rani loved Tingle Reef. The water was warm and crystal clear and the reef was full of friendly sea-creatures who all lived happily together in their colourful underwater home. It was the only home Rani could remember. She had been found as a baby by Kai's parents inside a Giant Clam-Shell at the edge of the reef. No one knew where Rani had come from and it was a mystery how she had got there. Kai's family had adopted Rani as their own. Rani felt that Murdoch and Miriam were the best parents she could wish for and that Kai was the best sister.

The only time she ever felt different was when anyone commented on her appearance.

Rani looked very different from the other mermaids. It wasn't just her hair. Her scales were a deep orange colour whereas all the other mermaids had green tails. Instead of having eyes that were sea-blue or sea-green, Rani had goldy-brown eyes. In fact, Rani's mother often joked that Rani didn't look like she came from the sea at all.

Kai suddenly stopped dead in mid tail-flip and Rani crashed right into her. She was looking at the rainbow fish, whose pink and yellow stripes made them the most colourful of all the fish in the reef.

"Look. There are the baby ones," Kai whispered to Rani, pointing at the tiny fish who had just hatched out of their eggs and were now swimming along beside their mothers. "Aren't they sweet?"

They watched happily until all the fish had swum by.

Then Rani noticed that the rock

where they had stopped to watch the fish was now far behind them. "We've drifted with the current," she said. "We're near the edge of the reef. We'd better swim back."

Kai and Rani were not allowed beyond the edge of the reef, where the sea dropped away suddenly to form the darker waters of the Deep Blue. It was easy to get lost in the strong sea currents, and fierce creatures lurked in the darkness beyond the reef. But this part of the reef was also scary for another reason. It was close to the Secret Cave.

The Secret Cave was somewhere on the edge of the Deep Blue. Long ago a strange mermaid called Morva had been banished to the cave after she had done something terrible using bad magic. Morva was known as the sea-witch. None of the mermaids liked to swim too near her cave, even though no one had seen her in years.

No other mermaid had ever been inside Morva's Secret Cave but Rani had heard stories about it since she was tiny. Its entrance was hidden by a magic bush that would catch you in its branches if you tried to swim through. The sea-witch used starfish as spies, so if anyone swam near her cave she would know they were coming. When the water at the edge of the reef got rough and murky, the mermaids said that Morva must be practising her sea-spells. Morva was said to be capable of changing the colour of the sea from turquoise to inky black if she lost her temper.

The more Rani thought about Morva, the more she wanted to leave quickly. "Come on," she urged her sister.

But before there was time for Kai to reply there was a terrible splashing and churning of water behind her and a crackly voice screeched, "What are you doing outside *my* cave?"

Chapter Two

Rani screamed. So did Kai.

Then came the sound of laughing and Rani saw that it was only the twins talking in cackly voices and hiding their faces behind some clumps of black seaweed.

"I am the sea-witch! I'm going to take you to my cave and turn you into a sea-frog!" Marissa hissed, as Marina rolled about in the water clutching her side from laughing so much.

"You should see your faces!"

Marina gasped.

Rani and Kai glared at the twins.

"What are *you* doing here?" Kai snapped.

"Look who's talking!" Marissa and Marina answered together. "What are *you* doing missing school?"

"We thought we'd follow you and see—" Marissa said.

"—what you were up to," Marina finished for her.

"You thought you'd spy on us, you mean," Kai retorted crossly. "You're worse than Morva's starfish, the way you spy on everyone!"

As the girls argued, Rani felt as though her body was filling up with pins and needles. The feeling seemed to start in her belly button and run up across her chest to her shoulders, then down her arms and into her hands. It was as though her fingers had an electric current in them as she held them out in front of her. She stared down at them but they didn't look any different. Then she was sure she heard a whispery voice calling her name. She closed her eyes tightly and shook her head.

"What's wrong with *you*?" the twins sniggered, staring at Rani.

Rani quickly opened her eyes. "Nothing," she said. "I thought I heard a strange voice, that's all."

"A *strange voice*?" Marina scoffed.

"Yes," said Kai, sounding scared. "I heard it too!"

Rani looked in amazement at her sister. "You did?"

"Of course. You don't think . . ." Kai looked frightened. "You don't think it really *could* be the sea-witch this time, do you?"

Marissa and Marina looked at each other, clearly having one of their private conversations just by thinking. Mermaid twins are able to read each others' thoughts, something which Marissa and Marina used to full advantage when they wanted to play tricks on people. Without saying another word, they swam off at high speed in the direction of home.

Rani turned to her sister to suggest they do the same, but Kai no longer looked scared. Instead she was laughing.

"Good one, Rani!" she said. "They really believed us!"

"But, Kai . . ." Rani stopped, starting to get a sick feeling in her stomach as she realized that Kai had only been trying to get her own back on the twins.

Her sister hadn't really heard the strange whispery voice at all.

*

The following day there was no school. Rani was washing out shell-dishes outside their cave while Kai was inside helping their mother cook lunch. Their father had gone to a special meeting of the community leaders earlier that morning and he had been gone for a very long time.

"Ouch!" Rani complained as she accidentally grazed her hand against the rocky wall of the cave.

Roscoe was bobbing about, peering into each shell to check for plankton. Plankton gets into everything, including all your shell-dishes, if you don't watch out.

He came over and had a look at Rani's hand. "Yuck!" he said. Roscoe was always squeamish at the sight of blood. Being a sea horse, he was lucky enough not to have any himself. "You've missed some sand in that one." He clanked his tail against the dish then ducked away from her and headed off in the direction of the shell-garden, which was his favourite place to relax.

"Mother, how come mermaid twins can read each others' thoughts?" Rani asked, as she carried the clean shell-dishes back into their cave. She made sure she hid her injured hand from her mother because she didn't want her to fuss.

Her mother stopped spreading plankton paste on to flat-weed cakes, turning so that her long golden hair swirled around her head. Rani's mother had the thickest, shiniest hair of all the mermaids, the most elegantly tapered tail, and her eyes were deep turquoise just like the sea out by the coral reef.

"You mean Marissa and Marina?" Rani nodded.

"Well, we don't really know. Some

identical twins are better at it than others."

"Are identical twins the only ones who can read minds?" Rani asked.

"As far as we know, yes. Except . . ." Her mother paused. "There are stories about mermaids long ago who could read the minds of all the other sea-creatures. Nobody knows if they really existed or whether people just made them up."

She reached out and smoothed down Rani's hair which had got tangled. Then she swam across the cave to check on Rani's baby sister, Pearl, who was fast asleep in her cradle, which was suspended from the ceiling. Their father had made the cradle out of one half of the Giant Clam-Shell that had brought Rani to them all those years ago.

Just then the seaweed door of their cave flapped open and their father swam in, followed by Kai. Murdoch's big powerful tail made the water in the cave churn so badly that Pearl's cradle rocked precariously.

"For goodness' sake, Murdoch! Please remember that this isn't the Deep Blue you're swimming in!" their mother said crossly.

"Sorry, Sweetheart!" Their father sat himself down on his favourite rock and wriggled until he got the end of his tail comfortably wedged into the sandy floor. Then he held out his arms for Rani and Kai to come and balance on his tail.

"Well, there haven't been any other sightings but we're going to send out a patrol this afternoon anyway," he told their mother, cheerfully.

"Sightings of *what*?" Kai asked.

"Someone *thought* they saw a Yellow-back jellyfish this morning inside the reef," he replied.

Yellow-back jellyfish lived in the Deep Blue and they were very dangerous indeed. They were so poisonous that no one had ever survived one of their stings. If anyone saw one inside the reef, the community always took it very seriously.

"It's probably a false alarm," Murdoch attempted to reassure them.

Rani frowned. "I don't think it is . . ." she said slowly.

Her mother looked at her sharply. "What do you mean?"

Rani shook her head. "I'm not sure. I just have this *feeling* . . ." She couldn't explain it any better than that. She stared down at her hands. They were starting to tingle again. And – as if by magic – the graze where she had bumped her hand against the rock had completely disappeared.

Chapter Three

"Roscoe, you've got to help me!" Rani pleaded, as she found the little sea horse sitting in the middle of the roundabout in the shell-garden. The roundabout was made out of one half of a huge cone shell with a flat surface of tight weeds netted over the top. It was balanced so that it spun on the ground on its point. Normally the mermaids would cling to the edge and be spun round together, but this afternoon the shell-garden was empty apart from the two of them.

"Push me round really fast and I'll think about it," Roscoe said.

"Roscoe, I think something strange is happening to me," Rani said, as she gave the roundabout a push. "Look at this." And she held out her healed hand for him to see.

As Roscoe passed he had a look. He spun round a couple more times and then jumped off. "Hmm. Very mysterious."

"And that's not all!" She told him about the whispery voices and the strange tingling sensation in her hands.

"Even more mysterious," Roscoe said. "Come on. You'd better come with me to see Octavius. He'll know what to do."

Octavius the octopus lived next door to the school cave – in fact it had been his idea to set up a school for the mermaid children in the first place. Octavius was always saying that just because mermaids had tiny brains that didn't mean they shouldn't fill them with as much knowledge as possible.

Octavius often complained about his

huge brain and how it tired him out thinking so many clever thoughts each day. For that reason he liked to take a nap every afternoon after lunch in order to keep his brain cells refreshed. None of the mermaid children were allowed to interrupt his naps and if they ever made too much noise outside his cave and woke him up then he was always very cross indeed.

Rani hung back. "But you know how grumpy Octavius gets when you ask him things."

"He only gets grumpy if you ask him things he doesn't know," Roscoe said. "Hurry up! We need to catch him before he goes to sleep for the afternoon."

"What if he doesn't know about *this*?"

Rani asked. "And what if he's already asleep?"

But Roscoe had already bobbed off in the direction of Octavius's cave.

The entrance to Octavius's cave was covered by a beautiful yellow and red seaweed-flap with sea anemones growing round the edges of the door.

Rani paused outside the cave. She knew she had to call out and say she was there, but she was too nervous to speak. Just as she was about to change her mind and go back, Roscoe knocked his bony tail loudly against the cave wall.

"Who's that?" a deep voice grumbled, and the seaweed-flap was pushed aside

by two long wriggly arms. Octavius
glared at them and Rani saw that
another arm held a shell-plate full of
delicious-looking food. He was washing
his cooking pots with another two arms
and with the remaining three he was
stuffing food into his mouth.

"As you can see, I'm very busy,"
Octavius snapped.

"This is Rani," Roscoe said, quickly.
"You know . . . *Rani*. The mermaid they
found in that shell."

"Ah . . . *Rani* . . ." Octavius said, and
he immediately stopped eating. He
pushed Roscoe out of the way with the
tip of one arm and put another arm
round Rani's shoulder. "Come in. Come
in," he said, pulling her towards him.

"I've been wondering when you'd come to see me."

Rani had never been inside Octavius's cave before. It was full of unusual things. There was a table in the middle of the floor made out of all different kinds of shells, and the stone floor was covered with a purple carpet of moss. Colourful plants were growing out of cracks in the cave walls and on one wall was a ridge cut into the stone on which were perched several books. To one side of the hot-rock stove lay a large flat cookery book, the pages of which were fluttering lightly with the movement of the water. Octavius had more books than anyone else Rani knew. Books in Tingle Reef

31

were very precious – they were made out
of the leaves of the book-plant which
was quite rare and could only be found
in the Deep Blue.

Octavius was clasping four of his arms
together in front of him, looking
thoughtful. "Well," he said, "so you're
ready, are you?"

"*Ready?*" Rani felt even more
confused. What was Octavius talking
about? She hadn't even told him yet why
she was here! She started to tell him
what had been happening but he cut her
short.

"I know all about that," he said. "It's
to be expected. After all, you're not a
Tingle Reef mermaid, are you? Now, the
only person who can explain things to

you properly is Morva."

"Morva, the *sea-witch*?" Rani gasped, open-mouthed.

"Don't tell me you believe all that mermaid nonsense! Morva is no more a sea-witch than . . ." He chuckled again. "Than *you* are!" He scratched his head and thought for a moment. "Now, you'll have to wait until I've finished my lunch. Come back in half an hour." And he started to wave Rani out of his cave.

Rani bravely stayed put. "Excuse me, Octavius, but what do you mean? Wait for *what*?"

"Why, for me to show you the way to Morva's cave of course," Octavius replied impatiently. "She's been expecting you for years!"

33

chapter four

Roscoe was waiting for her outside. "So?" he questioned her. "What did Mister Grumpy say, then?"

"Shush! He'll hear you," Rani hissed. "Roscoe, did you know that Octavius knows Morva?"

Roscoe looked surprised. "Does he?"

"Yes, and he *says* that she's the only one who can explain things to me."

Roscoe did a little dance. "I knew it! *You* must be a sea-witch too!"

"Don't be silly," Rani snapped. But all

the same, she could feel her heart beating faster.

Rani swam back to the shell-garden. She could hear Kai and the twins playing noisily on the seaweed swings. Kai always liked to prove that she could swing the highest and now her long blonde hair streamed out as she used her tail to push herself higher and higher.

Suddenly Kai swung so high that she was completely upside down and her shell-haircomb flew off. It landed in a huge bush of sea-kelp near Rani.

Rani swam over and started to rummage amongst the big fluttery leaves.

"There it is," she gasped, reaching down to grab at a shiny shell.

"Do you mind?" the shell said crossly,

and Rani let go of it with a gasp. It wasn't Kai's hair-comb but a live shell with a sea creature living inside it.

"Wow!" Kai said, joining her. "It's an oyster!"

"An oyster!" the twins exclaimed, hurrying over to look. "Has it got a pearl inside?"

"Have you got a pearl inside?" Kai

asked it, excitedly.

"Don't be so nosy," the oyster snorted. "You mermaids have no manners!"

"I'm sorry," Kai said. "It's just . . . I've never seen an oyster with a pearl and – if it's not too much trouble – we'd love to see one."

"It *is* too much trouble," the oyster snapped, opening slightly and rudely releasing an air bubble.

The twins went silent. At least, it seemed like they were being silent until Rani heard Marina's voice, faint and whispery, saying, "Let's wait until Rani and Kai have gone and then come back for it."

"You can't do that!" Rani said to them, sharply.

Kai gave her a strange look and so did the twins.

"We didn't say anything," Marina said cautiously. She looked at her twin to make sure that she hadn't accidentally spoken the words. "Did we, Marissa?"

Marissa shook her head, still staring at Rani. "We didn't *say* anything, no."

Kai was trying to win the oyster round by complimenting it on the shininess of its shell.

"Flattery will get you nowhere," the oyster said. "I know what you mermaids are like. If I show you my pearl you'll run off with it!"

"No, we won't," said Kai. "We promise we won't!"

"Hmm," said the oyster, shifting

himself to a more comfortable position in the sand. "I'll tell you what . . . I'll *describe* it to you."

And he went on to describe the biggest, smoothest, most beautiful pearl any mermaid could imagine.

"Oh, *please* can we see it?" begged Kai.

"I'm afraid not," said the oyster slyly. "But I have a cousin who lives under a rock just a short distance into the Deep Blue and *he* has a pearl that he loves to show to people. I can give you directions."

He told Kai to swim one hundred of her tail-lengths straight out from the entrance to the sea-snake burrow, then turn right at a big bush of sea-kelp, then swim to the rock straight ahead that had a purple bush to one side.

"Come on," said the twins excitedly. "Let's go now."

Rani suddenly spotted Kai's shell-comb. "Here!" she cried out triumphantly, scooping it up just as Roscoe appeared with the message that

Octavius was ready now.

"Ready for what?" Kai asked, carefully replacing her hair-comb.

Rani knew she couldn't tell. Not yet anyway.

Kai looked hurt when Rani told her that it was a secret.

"Don't be upset," Rani pleaded. "I'll tell you as soon as I can."

"You don't have to," Kai replied huffily. "I'm going with the twins to find this oyster." And she swam off after the twins, in the direction of the Deep Blue.

"Kai, don't leave the reef!" Rani called after her anxiously. "If Mother and Father find out, you'll get into trouble! And besides, it might be dangerous!"

But Kai didn't stop.

"I wouldn't worry about her," Roscoe said, gruffly. "Where *you're* going is far more dangerous!" And he gave her a nudge with his bony head in the direction of Octavius's cave.

chapter five

"I can give you directions from here,"
Octavius said, stopping as they reached
the edge of the reef.

"You want me to go into the Deep
Blue alone?" Rani said, shocked.
Octavius had already insisted that
Roscoe stay behind and they had left
him at the octopus's cave.

"I feel it is my duty not to put
myself at undue risk," Octavius
explained gravely. "After all, my great
brain is a very valuable asset to the

whole community."

Rani was sure that it was, but at the same time she was petrified by the idea of swimming off into the Deep Blue by herself. She had only been in the Deep Blue a few times before with her father who had made her stay very close by his side the whole time. Murdoch made many expeditions into the Deep Blue with the other mermen to collect medicine plants and food and other essential things and he had told them stories about the creatures that lived there. Rani knew that many were friendly like the dolphins and the whales but that others were dangerous, like the sharks and the giant sea-spiders who would catch you and eat you, and the

Yellow-back jellyfish who would kill you with one sting.

"Don't worry," Octavius said. "I've sent a starfish to tell Morva you're coming. She'll be looking out for you. Now, listen carefully. I'm going to tell you how to get to the Secret Cave . . ."

Octavius explained the secret route twice and made her repeat it after him. She was to look out for three landmarks: a craggy rock that was completely covered in limpets; a huge flowering sea-cactus; and a tall bush that pointed upwards in the shape of a needle.

"What if I can't find them?" Rani asked.

"You will," Octavius said. "And when you get there, I want you to give Morva this from me." He handed her a little shell-container. "Hurry now."

Rani looked out anxiously into the dark water of the Deep Blue. Plucking up all her courage, she thrashed her tail and propelled herself over the edge of the reef.

It was much darker in the deep water, and colder too. Rani shivered as she swam down deeper and deeper to reach the seabed. She saw the rock covered in limpets that Octavius had told her to look for and turned left straight after it just like Octavius had said. Then she started to look for a bushy sea-cactus with blue flowers. As she swam past it a shoal of rainbow fish scuttled out from underneath, making her jump.

"There's a shark about," they told her.
"Watch out."

Rani shivered, but it was too late to
turn back. She thanked them for the
warning and continued on her way.

After what seemed like a long time she
saw the needle-shaped bush standing on
its own in a sandy clearing on the seabed.
She had to start swimming upwards now,

Octavius had said. But how could a cave be situated *above* her? It had to be on the seabed or in a rock somewhere.

But since the bush was definitely pointing upwards she decided she had better do what Octavius had said. Then, all of a sudden, the way up was blocked. She stopped dead and looked above her.

In the water above her head was what looked like a huge flat rock stretching out in all directions as far as she could see. She started to swim downwards away from it, thinking that perhaps it wasn't a rock but some huge sea-creature, when she heard a whispery voice calling, "*Look above you, Rani!*"

She looked, and this time she spotted an opening in the rock. And from the opening, a rope of seaweed was dangling down.

Up and up the rope she climbed, through the dark vertical tunnel, until it finally came to an end and all of a sudden she was inside a beautiful underwater cave.

The water inside the cave was crystal clear and beautiful yellow and purple fish swam around playfully. In one corner, two bright orange lobsters were dozing, their large pincers draped lazily round each other. The walls of the cave were decorated with brightly coloured murals of different kinds of sea-creatures, including mermaids, swimming around amongst the pink and purple coral.

Rani turned to look at the wall behind her and gasped.

In the middle of the wall was a picture of a mermaid with red hair and an orange tail, swimming down into the centre of what looked like a burst of golden light!

Rani held in her breath as she swam closer to study the picture. Just as she was almost touching it she heard a noise behind her.

She turned to look. There, blocking the entrance to the cave, was the strangest mermaid she had ever seen.

"Hello, Rani," the mermaid said.

"Are you? Are you *Morva*?" Rani stammered.

The mermaid had dazzling orange

scales and red hair so long that it
reached the tip of her tail. Rani saw that
her eyes looked old and wise. But how
could this be Morva? Old mermaids had
white hair and wrinkled faces! And
Morva wasn't just old – she was ancient!

"Welcome to my floating cave,"
Morva said, smiling.

chapter Six

The shell-container Octavius had sent
turned out to be a portion of his
delicious stew. As Rani watched Morva
heating up the stew on top of her hot-
rock stove she tried not to think about a
story her grandmother used to tell her,
about a naughty little mermaid who ran
off on her own into the Deep Blue and
ended up becoming the tenderest
ingredient in a sea-witch's supper.

"I thought you'd look much older,"
Rani said shyly. "Like my grandmother.

She's got white hair."

"I expect I'm twice as old as your grandmother," Morva said. "But one of the advantages of being able to use magic is that you don't have to *look* older!"

Rani swallowed. "They said— They said you used *bad* magic."

Morva stopped stirring her stew, which seemed to be bubbling up to ten times the quantity as she chanted over it.

"Let me tell you what really happened," she said.

And Morva told her that she came from a different group of mermaids a long way away from here and that, when she was young, she had met a merman from Tingle Reef when she was out

exploring in the Deep Blue. The
merman had swum farther than usual
because he was searching for a rare type
of plant with healing powers. The plant
was needed urgently because the baby of
one of the community leaders was very
sick. Morva had helped him to find the
plant and they had returned to Tingle

Reef together. Morva and the merman, who was called Murdoch, fell in love.

"That's the same name as my father!" Rani interrupted her.

Morva just nodded and carried on.

Morva and Murdoch were very happy apart from one thing. There was another mermaid who was in love with Murdoch and she was very jealous of Morva. When the community leader's baby started to get sick again, Morva offered to make a magic healing potion but the jealous mermaid secretly substituted salt for the potion and the baby died. The jealous mermaid spread the rumour that Morva had used bad magic and Morva was banished. Murdoch tried to go with her but Morva knew he would be unhappy away from Tingle Reef so she wouldn't let him.

But instead of returning home Morva used her magic to create a special floating cave on the edge of the reef. That way she could stay and watch over Murdoch, who eventually did fall in love again with someone else and had a family. Morva made it her business to watch over them, staying in her secret cave for many years, until Murdoch finally died. Then, just as she was thinking about returning to her own people, she heard that a baby mermaid with an orange tail and red hair had arrived in Tingle Reef inside a shell.

"*Me!*" Rani gasped.

"Yes, and the grandson of *my*

Murdoch found you and adopted you."
She smiled. "And I decided to stay a
while longer until you grew old enough
for me to teach you how to use your
magic."

"*What* magic?" Rani exclaimed.

"What do you think that tingling
feeling is in your body? And how do you
think you can hear other creatures'
thoughts, if not by magic? It's very weak
at the moment, only just beginning to
show itself. But in a little while it will be
as powerful as mine, so it's very
important that you learn how to use it
properly."

"But how . . ." Rani trailed off. She
had so many questions to ask that she
didn't know where to start.

"I don't know how or why you came to Tingle Reef as a baby, Rani," Morva continued. "But what I do know is that you must have come from the same place as me. And we are different from the mermaids of Tingle Reef, not just because of how we look. We're different because we have magic powers that they don't have."

Rani felt dazed. "If this is true," she stammered. "Then . . . then you must know where I come from."

Morva pointed at the picture of the red-haired mermaid swimming through the burst of golden light. "That," she said, proudly, "is where you come from."

Rani stared at the picture. "But where is it? How do we get there?"

"One day, when your magic is strong enough, I will take you there," Morva said. "Until then you must be patient."

Morva started to tuck into her stew. "Now you must go. You mustn't tell *anyone* that you have met me. Or about what I have told you. Do you understand?"

Rani nodded. "But when will I see you again?"

"Soon. And remember . . . Tell *no one*! Not even your family."

Rani took one last look at the picture, and as she left Morva's cave she tried to imagine herself swimming down through the centre of that golden light to reach her true home.

Chapter Seven

By the time Rani got back to Tingle Reef she felt exhausted. All she wanted to do was to go home and tell her parents and Kai all about it, but she knew she couldn't. Rani *really* wanted to tell Kai. Surely it wouldn't matter if she made Kai promise not to tell anyone else?

As the entrance to her cave came into view, Rani saw that there were lots of other mermaids outside.

"What's happened?" she asked anxiously, as the crowd parted to let her through. Everyone was looking really worried.

As she swam inside, her mother looked up. She was hugging Pearl tightly and her turquoise eyes were full of tears. At first Rani thought there was something wrong with her baby sister and then she spotted her father.

Murdoch was lying on a seaweed mat, completely still.

"What's wrong with Father?" she cried.

"He's been stung by a Yellow-back jellyfish," her mother replied, her voice trembling.

Rani looked down at Murdoch. The jellyfish poison was already in his bloodstream and his upper body was red and swollen. His eyes were closed and he was so weak he couldn't move his tail.

"Rani, isn't Kai with you?" her mother asked.

Rani shook her head. "She went somewhere with the twins."

"Where?"

Rani knew that if she told her mother

63

that Kai had gone off into the Deep
Blue then her mother would be even
more worried. So she lied. "She's not far
away. Shall I go and fetch her?"

"Yes," her mother said hoarsely. She
touched Murdoch's forehead. "But
hurry!"

Rani swallowed, fighting back the
tears. Her mother expected that her
father would die. That was why she
wanted Kai to come back so quickly.

"Mother—" she began, but Miriam
interrupted her.

"There's no cure for this type of
poison, Rani. Now go and fetch your
sister."

Rani swam out of the cave and found
Roscoe.

"Roscoe, will *you* go and find Kai?"
Rani asked. "There's somewhere else
I need to go right now." And she
swam away before he could ask her any
questions.

Rani swam as fast as she could back to
Morva's cave.

When she reached it, she swam
underneath it until she found the hole
with the seaweed rope.

"Morva," she gasped, as soon as she
was inside the cave. "You've got to help
me!"

Morva was sitting on the furthest away
rock, combing her long hair with a
beautiful shell-comb. She stopped as
soon as she saw Rani.

Rani quickly explained what had

happened to her father.

Morva looked distressed. "I'd like to help," she said. "I could collect some special plants and make a magic healing potion to give you. You can come back and collect it tonight."

"There isn't time for that!" Rani cried desperately. "Father's going to die if you don't come and do something now."

"But Rani, I cannot enter Tingle Reef," Morva said. "It is forbidden. They will never permit me to go into the cave to help your father."

"They will if I take you!" Rani said. "Morva, please, you've got to come."

Morva looked solemn. "I can't. They still think I killed that baby."

"Well, this is your chance to show

everybody that they're wrong," Rani said. "If you make Father better then they'll know you couldn't have killed anyone." Rani was near to tears now. "Murdoch would want you to come!" she burst out. "*Your* Murdoch, I mean. Can't you just try?"

When they got back to Rani's cave some of the other mermaids were still outside. They gasped as they saw Morva. Most of them didn't know who she was, but a few of the older mermaids remembered her from when *they* were children.

An urgent whisper went round. "It's Morva! It's the sea-witch!"

The adult mermaids moved closer

together, blocking the entrance to the cave.

"That child looks just like the sea-witch!" one of them said, pointing at Rani's bright red hair.

"Shhh. You'll frighten Rani," another mermaid said protectively.

Morva looked at Rani. "I knew they wouldn't understand," she said. "I'd better leave."

"But you have to save Father!" Rani cried. "You have to come inside and see him." And she burst into tears.

At that moment Octavius pushed his way through the crowd, shoving mermaids out of his way, eight-at-a-time, until he reached Rani.

"Rani has brought Morva here to help

Murdoch!" he shouted, hooking one arm round Rani's waist and pulling her closer to him. "And since we can't help him ourselves, I don't think we've got anything to lose by letting Morva try, do you?"

"But she's dangerous!" someone shouted. "What about what she did to that baby?"

"Nonsense!" Octavius snorted. "You mermaids are *so* silly! I've read all about what happened in my history book of Tingle Reef. No one ever listened to Morva's side of the story. Unfortunately I hadn't been born then or I would have sorted it all out! Now, move aside and let Rani and Morva enter the cave."

But the adult mermaids didn't move. They didn't like being bossed around by Octavius.

Rani was getting scared that they wouldn't reach her father in time. She tugged at Morva's arm. "*Do* something!"

Morva seemed to whirl into action, flicking her tail so that the water swirled around her. "If you don't move out of the way I'm going to turn you all into sea-frogs!" she hissed. And she started to wave her arms in the water in front of her as if she was casting a spell.

The mermaids started pushing and shoving each other as they struggled to move away from her. Quickly, Morva pushed Rani ahead of her into the cave.

"Mother!" Rani called out from the doorway.

Rani's mother turned round. "Rani—" She stopped, gasping out loud and pulling Pearl closer to her, as she saw Morva.

"Morva is my friend," Rani said. "And she's come to make Father better."

Before her mother could say anything Morva swam forward. "I *can* help him," she said. "*If* you trust me."

"I've heard about you," Rani's mother whispered. "But I never guessed that you . . . that Rani . . ." She trailed off, her gaze flitting between Morva's long red hair and the identical red hair of her daughter.

"There isn't much time," Morva said gently.

Rani's mother looked down at her husband. She kissed his forehead and moved back.

"Go on, then," she said.

Morva swam closer and leaned over Murdoch. She placed both hands, fingers outstretched, over his face. Then she closed her eyes and began to chant something under her breath. As Miriam and Rani watched, Morva's upper body began to sparkle. The golden glow started to spread down her arms and into her hands and then it crossed over into Murdoch's body which started to sparkle too.

Slowly, the redness left his skin and the swelling started to go down. The end of his tail started to twitch. When Morva removed her hands, the golden light vanished and Murdoch's eyes flickered open.

Rani's mother was trembling. "Oh, thank you!" she cried. "Thank you so much!" She rushed forward and flung her arms around her husband, as Pearl shrieked with excitement.

Rani flung herself at Morva and gave her an enormous hug. "I knew you'd save him!"

Suddenly there was a lot of noise at the cave entrance and Kai swam inside with Roscoe, closely followed by Octavius.

"What is it? What's happening?" Kai asked.

"It's all right now," her mother told her, smiling. "Murdoch is all right now. Thanks to Morva."

"Morva?" Kai stared at the beautiful red-haired mermaid who was holding Rani's hand. "*You're* Morva? But . . . but Morva's meant to be *ugly*!"

Morva laughed, sending golden bubbles spiralling above her head.

"*Kai!*" her mother snapped, but she was too happy to be very cross.

One by one the other mermaids started to come inside the cave to see what Morva had done. When they saw Murdoch sitting up on the mat, they all stared at him in awe.

"Maybe Octavius was right," they mumbled. "Maybe she *didn't* kill that baby."

"Of *course* I was right!" Octavius barked at them. "I'm *always* right. When are you mermaids going to realize that?"

"Of *course* Morva didn't kill that baby," Murdoch called out. "My grandfather was always telling you that, but you never listened!"

All the mermaids stared in admiration at Morva.

"You can come back and live in

Tingle Reef now," Rani told her
excitedly.

"Yes, Morva!" one or two of the other
mermaids called out. "Come and live
here with us."

Morva smiled but she shook her head.
"Thank you, I'm very happy living in my
floating cave. But I'd like to come and
visit you. It gets a bit lonely sometimes,
with no other mermaids to talk to."

"Come and visit us whenever you
want!" everyone said at once.

And Morva promised them that she
would.

Chapter Eight

"Do you think Morva will come?" Kai asked Rani, as they waited for their father's speech to finish.

It was market day and Murdoch was giving a talk to the community about the seaweed nets they were going to use in future to catch any dangerous jellyfish. The one that had stung Murdoch had been sent back into the Deep Blue but there was always a risk that another Yellow-back might find its way inside the reef.

The market had been in full swing all morning with all sorts of different goods being exchanged. There were lots of delicious things to eat as well as practical things for the home like seaweed mats and shell-crockery. Things had quietened down a bit now that a lot of the stall-holders and shoppers had gathered round to hear what Murdoch had to say.

"Are you sure Morva's coming?" Kai asked her sister again.

"Yes, she'll be here. She's just a bit late, that's all," Rani replied.

"She'd *better* come, after all the time we've spent making this." Kai opened the little shell-box she was holding and the girls looked down again at the beautiful pearl necklace inside.

"I can't believe that oyster you and the twins found actually *gave* you his pearl," Rani said.

"He said he was getting bored with it," Kai explained. "He was extremely happy when I gave him my shell-comb and all my jewellery in exchange for it."

"Are you sure you want *me* to make the presentation?" Rani asked. "After all, it's your pearl."

"I think it's best if you do it," Kai said. "Anyway, she'll know it's from all of us."

Just then Octavius appeared, carrying a seaweed shopping bag in each arm. "I've got so much shopping to do that I don't know whether I'm coming or going," he grumbled.

Someone cried, "Morva's here!"

Rani and Kai looked up. Morva was swimming towards them, her long red hair streaming out behind her.

Murdoch beckoned to Rani to come over to the big rock platform in the middle of the marketplace.

"Here," Kai whispered, handing her the little shell-box.

The whole crowd fell silent as they waited for Murdoch to speak.

"We're very pleased to welcome Morva here today," Murdoch announced. "Morva, I want to thank you once again for saving my life, and Rani has something to give you from all of us."

Rani swam over to Morva and presented her with the little shell-box. Morva opened it and gasped with pleasure as she saw the necklace.

"It's beautiful," she said. "Thank you *so* much."

"Welcome back to Tingle Reef!" Rani said, and everyone cheered.

The excitement died down considerably as Octavius climbed up on to the platform. "If *I* could just add a few words . . ." he began.

The mermaids sighed as they prepared themselves for what they knew was bound to be a very long speech indeed.

That's when Rani noticed that little gold sparks were starting to dance around Octavius's mouth. She looked suspiciously at Morva whose fingertips were giving off a faint glow.

"That's all I have to say!" Octavius said grandly. And, much to everyone's amazement, he climbed straight down again from the platform.

All the mermaids started to clap.

"You see, Rani," Morva's whispery words came floating towards her through the water. "Mermaid magic can sometimes come in *very* useful indeed!"

Mermaids

Rani's Sea Spell

For Rani and Sunil

chapter one

Rani and her family were having
breakfast. The water in their cave was
lovely and warm because the hot-rock
stove was on and Roscoe, Rani's pet
sea horse, was floating lazily next to it.

They all jumped as a huge fishy nose
pushed itself through the seaweed-flap
that covered the cave entrance.

"It's Pat!" Rani and her sister, Kai, left
their breakfast and swam over to greet
the big grey dolphin who was now half
in and half out of the cave. Pat brought

87

them messages from outside Tingle Reef.

"Is everything all right?" asked their mother, who was sitting on the seaweed mat feeding their baby sister, Pearl, with a tiny shell-spoon.

"Everything is fine," Pat reassured her. "I've brought you an invitation. Your mother wants you all to visit them next week. They're throwing a grand party!"

Rani's grandmother didn't live in Tingle Reef. She lived inside a shipwreck in the Deep Blue. Rani's mother had lived there when she was a child and had told them lots of exciting stories about it.

"A party!" shouted Kai. "Oh, please can we go, Mother?"

Rani and Kai had never been to their grandmother's home before. You had to swim far into the Deep Blue to get there and, until now, their parents had always said that they were too young to make the trip.

"Well . . ." Miriam looked at her husband, clearly excited by the idea of the party as well. "What do you think, Murdoch?"

Their father looked thoughtful. "I think Kai and Rani probably *are* old enough to go this time, but we should get someone to look after Pearl."

"*YES!*" shouted Rani and Kai together, clasping hands and swishing their tails in unison as they propelled themselves excitedly round the cave.

"Come in and have some breakfast with us, Pat," Murdoch said, but the

dolphin replied that he had several more messages to deliver.

"But I'll tell them to expect you at the party!" he said, giving them his biggest dolphin grin as he backed out of the cave.

Rani couldn't wait to tell her friend, Morva, about the party. Morva was

known in Tingle Reef as the sea-witch
because she was very old and wise and
she could do magic. Morva's magic was
always good – but some of the other
mermaids were afraid of her. She lived
in a special floating cave in the Deep
Blue, just outside Tingle Reef, and Rani
often went to visit her there.

Rani and Morva weren't like the other
mermaids. Instead of having blonde hair
and green tails like the others, they had
red hair and orange tails. Morva's hair
was so long that it touched the tip of her
tail. And even though she was very old –
almost ancient – Morva still looked
young and beautiful.

There was a special reason why Rani
was such a frequent visitor to Morva's

cave – a reason that most of the other mermaids didn't know about. Rani had recently discovered that she too had magic powers, and now Morva was teaching her how to make them stronger.

As Rani swam out through the Deep Blue towards Morva's floating cave, all she could think about was the party and what she was going to wear. She had some special shell-combs which she could put in her hair and some glitter-sand to make her hair sparkly . . .

Rani found the cave floating in its usual place, past the bushy sea-cactus with the blue flowers and straight up from the needle-shaped bush. She swam through the opening in the magic rock, grabbed hold of the seaweed rope and hauled herself up the narrow vertical tunnel that led inside.

"Wow!" she gasped, as she entered Morva's cave. The water inside the floating cave was usually crystal clear, but today Morva had changed the colour to pink with one of her sea-spells.

Morva beckoned for Rani to come and join her. Although Morva's face was young and beautiful, her eyes were old and wise. She was sitting on a rock with her long red hair billowing out around her as she listened to two lobsters playing a duet on some shell-horns. When they had finished, Rani joined in Morva's clapping.

"I taught them that melody myself," Morva said. "Now, Rani . . . Let's see

what I can teach *you* today."

Neither Morva or Rani had been
born in Tingle Reef. Rani had been
found as a baby and adopted by Miriam
and Murdoch. They had found her
inside a Giant Clam-Shell on the edge of
the reef and nobody knew how she had
got there. Morva had come to Tingle
Reef long before Rani's parents – or

even her grandparents – had been born.
She came from a community of magic
mermaids who lived in a secret place
far away and Morva had promised
that one day she would take Rani there –
but first Rani had to learn a lot more
magic.

Before Rani had time to tell her about
the party, Morva was swimming about
the cave looking for something. "We
need something to mend. Aah! This will
do." She lifted up a delicate shell-dish
and banged it against the cave wall so
that it broke into several pieces. "Right,"
said Morva briskly. "What have I told
you about starting up magic?"

"You have to *think* it up inside your
head," said Rani, as she desperately tried

to stop thinking about glitter-sand and shell-combs.

"Exactly. Which means you have to concentrate very hard indeed, so close your eyes . . ."

Rani closed her eyes and tried to focus on the mending spell but all she could think about was her grandmother's party.

Morva peered at her more closely. "You're very excited about something. What is it?"

And at last Rani was able to tell her about the dolphin's visit that morning.

"Well, that *is* exciting," replied Morva. "Now let me think . . ." She looked thoughtful. "I know! I will give you a special sea-spell to take with you on your journey."

"What sort of spell?" asked Rani eagerly. "What does it do?"

"Before I tell you that," Morva said, "I need to be sure that you can concentrate hard enough to make the spell work."

"Of course I can!" Rani burst out. To prove it, she closed her eyes and started to concentrate again on the mending spell, picturing the broken pieces of shell-dish coming back together again. She could feel a tingling sensation starting up in her belly button and spreading upwards. Soon her fingertips felt warm. She opened her eyes and saw that they were glowing. Slowly, she spread out her fingers above the broken pieces of shell.

"Well done!" Morva smiled.

The shell-dish was all in one piece again, surrounded by a golden glow.

Rani grinned. "I did it!"

Morva nodded, still smiling. "Now, let me tell you about my special sea-spell . . ."

Chapter Two

On the morning they were due to set off for the shipwreck, Rani and her family got up very early indeed. The shipwreck was a long way away and it would take them most of the day to get there.

As they got ready, there was a knock at the door of their cave.

"That will be Morva," their mother said. Morva had offered to look after Pearl while they were gone.

"Come in!" everyone shouted, and Morva swam inside the cave, her red hair streaming out behind her.

"Octavius is here too," Morva said.

Octavius, the octopus, followed her into the cave. He had tied two of his long wriggly arms together to make a loop and hanging from the loop were lots of shell-containers and bulky seaweed bags.

"Pat told me about the party and I'm

coming too. My sister, Flora, lives on the shipwreck," Octavius explained. "I can't think why she didn't send me an invitation!"

"Why are you taking so much stuff?" asked Kai.

"Ah, well . . . That's the trouble with having a huge brain like mine – one thinks of so many things to pack." He sighed as he readjusted some of his bags.

"I didn't know your sister lived on the wreck," Rani said.

"Oh, yes. Flora works there as a hairdresser," Octavius told her.

"Maybe we'll ask her to do our hair for the party," Rani's mother said, as she swam over to make sure they were ready. "Now, have you girls got your seaweed belts tied nice and tightly?"

Rani and Kai nodded. They each had a packed lunch tied to their belts, and a little purse containing the jewellery and hair decorations they were going to wear at the party.

"We'd better get going," said Murdoch.

"Bye-bye, Pearl," the girls said, rushing to give their baby sister a final hug. "We wish you were coming with us."

"Pearl will be just fine with me," Morva reassured them, as Pearl beamed happily at everybody from Morva's arms.

Just as they were leaving, Morva fastened a gold-coloured shell to Rani's belt. "The sea-spell is inside," Morva whispered. "And remember – it can only be used once, so don't use it unless you really have to!"

Rani promised that she wouldn't, as she gave Morva a goodbye hug.

They swam through the Deep Blue for a long time, with Murdoch leading the way. Rani and Kai swam behind him, with Octavius and Miriam swimming behind the girls. Every time Roscoe got tired he grabbed hold of one of the mermaids' hair and caught a ride with them for a while until he felt like swimming again.

The water in the Deep Blue was darker and colder than the water in

Tingle Reef. The further out they swam, the more strange the plants and rocks that surrounded them. Rani and Kai, who had never been this far out in the Deep Blue before, couldn't stop pointing things out to each other.

"Look!" gasped Kai, as a shoal of enormous fish swam by. Murdoch explained that a lot of the fish in the

Deep Blue were bigger than the ones they were used to seeing at home.

"Octavius, what have you *got* in those bags?" Kai asked the octopus, as they rested at the bottom of a large rock to eat their packed lunches. Murdoch was sitting on top of the rock acting as look-out.

"I have brought some of my famous stew for the party," Octavius said grandly, "since I know how much everyone likes it."

"Yes, but you don't eat *stew* at a party," Kai pointed out. "You eat mer-cakes and sea-trifle and—"

"What's that noise?" her mother interrupted.

There was a definite banging noise

that seemed to be coming from very close by.

"Murdoch!" Miriam called up to him, anxiously. "Can you come down here?"

"What's wrong?" Murdoch asked, swimming down to join them. Then he heard the noise too.

"There's a creature inside that rock. I can sense it," Rani said, frowning. Rani's magical powers often helped her to sense the presence of other creatures before they appeared.

Her family looked at her in disbelief. How could a creature be *inside* a rock? "I'm going to have a look," Rani said, swimming away from the others before they could stop her.

As she swam round to the other side

of the rock she noticed a bush growing out of it. The bush was swishing from side to side even though the water here was quite calm.

"Rani!" Her father appeared by her side just as a huge fish with sharp fins, a jagged tail, a huge mouth and very sharp teeth indeed, swam out from behind the bush.

"*SHARK!*" yelled Murdoch, pulling Rani behind him.

Rani started to fumble for the little golden shell that Morva had fastened to her belt – the shell with the sea-spell. But in her panic, the shell slipped from her fingers and floated away from her.

The huge shark was heading straight towards them, its white teeth flashing.

Then it seemed to sniff something it liked better. It batted Murdoch and Rani to one side and swam past them, heading straight for the others.

Rani and her father yelled out a warning, but it was too late. The shark had already trapped Miriam, Kai, Octavius and Roscoe. As they trembled against the rock face, the shark's evil black eyes glinted in pleasure at the prospect of such a yummy dinner.

That's when Rani heard the shark's thoughts floating towards her through the water. Rani's magic meant that she could often hear the thoughts of other sea creatures. The shark was smelling a mixture of mermaids and . . .

"Octavius! Throw him your stew!"

Rani shouted. "That's what he can smell!"

Octavius hastily untied his arms and pushed all the containers of stew towards the shark's open mouth. As the shark started to crunch it up greedily, Octavius and the others slipped past to join Murdoch and Rani.

"Quick!" said Murdoch urgently. "It won't take him long to get through that lot."

"Where's Rani going?" Kai asked suddenly.

Rani was swimming away from them, back towards the bush which had concealed the entrance to the shark's cave. "I have to get Morva's shell!" she called back. "You go on. I'll catch up with you in a minute!"

Rani spotted the shell straight away, gleaming up at her from a bunch of dark green seaweed. She picked it up and fastened it securely to her belt just as Murdoch caught up with her. He grabbed her firmly by the arm.

"I'm sorry, Father, but this shell is important," Rani said.

"So are you!" snapped her father. "Now, just *swim*! Before that shark realizes that the stew he's munching doesn't contain any mermaids at all!"

Chapter Three

"It's not far now," Miriam said, when Rani and Kai started to protest that they were getting tired. As they swam over a sandy opening in the rocks where lots of colourful fish darted about, Miriam became excited. "I recognize where we are! We're nearly there." She started to swim faster. "Look." She pointed ahead. "There it is!"

Rani and Kai looked ahead of them and couldn't believe what they were seeing. Even the descriptions their mother had given them hadn't prepared them for *this*.

Towering up from the seabed was the strangest structure they had ever seen. As they swam closer they saw that it was white because it was totally covered in limpet shells. There were many openings along the sides of the vessel – entrances to individual homes with colourful plants and flowers growing around the doorways. On top was a massive roof garden which stretched out over the whole area of the wreck. The garden was filled with all sorts of flowering shrubs and plants. Seaweed hammocks, strung up between the bushes, were swinging in the gentle current and there were lots of rock seats dotted here and there amongst the greenery. Some mermaids, who were relaxing in the garden, smiled and waved to them.

"It's beautiful!" gasped Kai and Rani together, as they waved back.

"Miriam!" someone called.

They turned to see an old mermaid with white hair swimming towards them.

"Mother!" cried Miriam, rushing forward.

The girls swam forward too, and soon their grandmother was hugging them tightly as she stroked their hair and told them how much they'd grown.

As everyone swam inside, Octavius asked about his sister Flora.

"She's very busy doing everyone's hair for the party tonight. Come with me and

I'll show you where we're having it."
Rani's grandmother led the way along
narrow corridors until they reached a
huge room with a tall ceiling and large
openings on both sides so that you could
see out into the Deep Blue in both
directions.

"It looks wonderful!" enthused
Miriam.

Rani thought it did too. A stone table along one side of the room was piled high with shell-dishes in readiness for the party. In one corner, a stage had been erected for the band. Purple and red seaweed decorations swung from the ceiling and the floor was sprinkled with glitter-sand.

"Hmm," murmured Octavius, who had swum up to inspect the ceiling and was now poking at it with the ends of his wriggly arms. "This ceiling is sagging."

"I don't see it," said Rani's grandmother sharply.

"Well, it is," said Octavius soberly. "You realize that if the ceiling collapsed, the whole roof garden would fall on top of us." He paused so that everyone could imagine being crushed by the roof garden, before adding, "Of course, I expect it's safe enough for the time being." He swam down to join them. "Now, I really must go and see my sister."

"Ask her if she'll do our hair too," Rani's mother called after him.

Octavius waved one arm at her to show that he would, as he swam off muttering under his breath. Really, it was hopeless trying to get mermaids to think about anything but their hair! They *meant* well, but they were such silly, scatty creatures. Still, he supposed it wasn't really their fault they had such tiny brains – unlike *his* which felt so heavy these days that he was beginning to wonder if it was *growing*! He must ask Flora what she thought. Now . . . where was she? He couldn't wait to see the surprise on her face when she saw him!

"You both look lovely," Rani's grandmother said, as she watched her two granddaughters get dressed up for the party. "Now . . . I have a surprise for you."

The girls gasped as she opened the lid of an old wooden box to reveal all sorts of necklaces and bracelets and rings.

"This is my treasure chest," said their grandmother. "Whatever you choose from it to wear tonight is yours to keep, so choose carefully."

"Oh, Grandmother!" cried Rani, her

eyes shining with excitement. "They're all beautiful."

"Especially this," said Kai, picking out a necklace of aquamarine that matched her eyes. "May I *really* have it?"

Her grandmother nodded. "And what about you, Rani? What will you choose?"

Rani's gaze fell on a simple pendant made out of a large amber stone. She picked it up.

"Ah, the amber pendant . . ." said her grandmother. "I found that one day when I was out looking for some special plants to make up some medicines. It was just lying there on the seabed. And the same day, Pat, the dolphin arrived and told me that your mother and father

had found a baby that morning, inside a Giant Clam-Shell."

"So we both got found on the same day!" Rani said, carefully fastening the pendant round her neck.

"It's glowing!" Kai gasped.

Rani looked down at the pendant. The amber stone really did seem to be lit from the inside now that it was touching Rani's skin.

"Let me try it on," Kai said.

The girls swapped necklaces but for some reason the pendant looked quite dull and ordinary on Kai.

"I like mine better," said Kai, quickly swapping back.

"Ah, here comes our hairdresser," said their grandmother, as a loud jangling noise attracted her attention.

Sure enough, the noise was Octavius's sister, Flora, who wore several bangles on each arm which clinked against each other as she moved about.

"Did Octavius find you?" Rani asked, excitedly. "I bet you weren't expecting him, were you? Did you get a lovely surprise when you saw him?"

"No, I certainly *wasn't* expecting him," said Flora, creasing her large forehead into a very wrinkly frown. "I've never been so—" She gave a polite cough as Octavius followed her into the room, ". . . so *surprised* in my life!"

"Nobody minds if I watch, do they?" Octavius asked, settling himself on the most comfortable-looking rock.

Since Flora had eight arms to work with, she could do marvellous things with mermaids' hair, very quickly indeed. Even Octavius was forced to admire the speed with which his sister combed and curled and crimped the long mermaid strands.

"If only I didn't have *red* hair," Rani sighed, as she waited for Flora to finish. Flora was using some of her arms as curlers in Kai's hair, so she only had three arms free to work on Rani. Octavius was suggesting ways his sister could use her arms even more efficiently as she wove Rani's hair into a long plait.

"I've only ever seen one other mermaid before who looked like you," Flora said, as she fixed Rani's shell-clasp

in place. "She had hair the same colour as yours and she was very beautiful. She told me she came from a secret place a long way away."

"You're talking about Morva," Octavius interrupted impatiently. "We all know her."

"This wasn't Morva," Flora said.

"Morva's ancient. This was a young mermaid. She had eyes just like yours, Rani, and she wore a pendant just like that one. She was resting in a cave because she was about to have a baby. Her husband had gone to look for food. I offered to do her hair for her. I couldn't resist – it was so beautiful."

"Where did you see her?" Rani gasped. "*When* was this? Did she tell you her name? Did she—"

"Oh, I can't remember the details," Flora interrupted. "It was about ten years ago. It was out in the Deep Blue somewhere."

"Flora – you've never told me any of this before!" Octavius said crossly. "This is very important information. How can

124

you forget to mention something like this?"

Flora started to jangle her bangles in an irritated manner. "I probably wasn't speaking to you at the time," she snapped back. "Since you were just as much of a know-all ten years ago as you are now!"

"Well, really," Octavius snorted, and the two octopuses started to bicker loudly.

Rani was stunned. Flora had met a red-haired mermaid with a pendant just like hers! And that mermaid had been about to have a baby – a baby who would be Rani's age by now! What if . . . What if . . . What if the mermaid Flora had met had been Rani's true mother?

Chapter Four

There was no time to ask Flora any more questions because by the time she had finished arguing with Octavius, it was almost time for the party to begin. But she promised to come and find Rani later so they could talk some more.

As the mermaids gathered together in the big hall, chattering excitedly, Rani thought that they all looked beautiful. Their long hair had been dressed up by Flora and decorated with shell-combs and flowers, and they all wore lovely jewellery made from shells or precious stones. The mermen looked very handsome too, with garlands of twisted leaves on their heads and colourful seaweed belts.

The band was the biggest Rani had ever seen. Mermaids and mermen were playing shell-horns, flutes and drums of all different kinds. There was even a harp with bind-weed strings. But Rani's favourite thing was the glocken-shell – an instrument made up of lots of different-sized shells, each one sounding a different note when it was played.

Rani was scanning the room for Flora. Flora had said she was coming to the party too, when she had finished doing everyone's hair. Where was she?

"First, everyone must have a turn at singing," announced Rani's grandmother.

Mermaids were known for their beautiful voices and most of them loved to sing, but Rani had always felt far too shy to sing in front of other people.

Rani's mother sang first. She had a particularly lovely voice and everyone had tears in their eyes as they listened. Rani really wished that she could sing like that. As the other mermaids took their turns Rani started to feel nervous. She had to be the only mermaid whose voice always trembled whenever she tried to sing. What would the others think of her?

"Rani, it's your turn now!" her

grandmother said.

Rani was about to make an excuse when she happened to glance down at her pendant. It made her happy just to look at it and suddenly she felt like she could do anything if she really wanted to! She swam up on to the stage and – much to her amazement – found herself able to sing after all. In fact, she sang so beautifully that the whole room clapped and cheered when she had finished.

"I never knew you could sing like that," whispered Kai afterwards.

"Neither did I," gasped Rani, touching the pendant in awe. She was about to say more about it to Kai when their grandmother announced that it was time to have supper.

Rani and Kai swam to the table to choose what they wanted from the delicious spread of mer-cakes and sea-trifles and ocean-fruits. The grown-up mermaids were drinking lots of mer-wine and getting very merry indeed.

"This is yummy. Not a bit of seaweed in sight!" laughed Kai, who was always being told off for not eating her greens.

"And no stew either!" laughed Rani. Suddenly she spotted Flora across the other side of the room. "I'll be back in a minute," she told her sister.

"Wait, Rani! Where's your necklace?" asked Kai, seeing that it was gone from Rani's neck.

Rani looked down. "Oh, no! It must have fallen off."

At that moment, Rani was surrounded by a group of mermaids who demanded that she sing for them again. Rani protested that she had to find her necklace first, but the others were very excited and wouldn't take no for an answer.

"Don't be a spoilsport, Rani!" her grandmother called out from the other side of the room.

Rani didn't know what to do. She couldn't tell her grandmother that she had lost the necklace, but how else could she explain that she didn't want to sing without it?

"I'll look for it," offered Kai. "Give them one song and then come and help me. Don't worry. It's got to be here *somewhere*. It must be."

Reluctantly, Rani agreed but as she took her place on the stage again, she had a horrible thought. What if it was the pendant that had given her the ability to sing before? What if now – without it – she was just as hopeless as ever? Rani's throat felt tight. Her stomach started to churn. She was sure that her voice would come out totally shaky and everyone would laugh at her. She quickly mumbled something about a sore throat and left the stage.

"I *can't* sing without my pendant," she told Kai.

"Maybe it fell off when you went to get your food," Kai said.

They swam back over the top of the

long table and looked in between all the dishes but they couldn't see the necklace.

Rani felt like crying.

"Don't worry. You can share *my* necklace," Kai said, putting her arm round her sister. "Or maybe Grandma has another one you can have."

But Rani knew that the amber pendant was far too special to be replaced.

"I've *got* to find it," she told Kai.

And together, the two sisters started to search again.

chapter five

It was getting late and Rani was starting
to feel sleepy. She still hadn't found her
pendant although she and Kai had
searched the whole room. She kept
checking to make sure that the little shell
containing the sea-spell was still fastened
to her belt.

Flora seemed to have disappeared
from the party. Rani was just giving up
all hope of speaking to her again when
she heard an unmistakable jangling
sound right behind her.

"Flora," Rani gasped. "I've been looking for you everywhere!"

"I've been avoiding Octavius," Flora confided. "He's just so *bossy*. It's just as well I don't live in Tingle Reef or he'd drive me mad!"

"He drives us mad too sometimes," Rani grinned. "But we know he always *means* well!"

The party had livened up even more since Octavius had suggested they dance a few reels. The mermaids were swishing their tails as fast as they could in time to the music as they held hands and swung each other round. Octavius was dancing with eight mermaids at once and looking very pleased with himself.

"It's getting very noisy," Flora said. "I

hope we don't upset our neighbours."

"What neighbours?" asked Rani.

Suddenly, as if in answer to her
question, an incredible bellow sounded.

"Oh dear," Flora said, looking out
into the Deep Blue with a worried frown
on her face.

"What is it?" asked Rani anxiously.

Flora pointed out into the dark water

which had suddenly become very choppy, and Rani saw an enormous black-and-white whale charging towards them.

"Whales have got very sensitive hearing," Flora whispered. "She's probably come to complain about the noise."

The furious whale banged against the side of the wreck and everyone stopped dancing.

The other mermaids made way for Rani's grandmother as she swam to the edge of the room so that she was looking out at the whale through a gap in the side of the wreck. "We're *terribly* sorry for disturbing you," she began, politely. "Can we make up for it by offering you some refreshments?" She looked across to the table where Octavius was helping himself to the last of the trifle. "We have lots of mer-wine and sea-fruits and—"

"I only eat plankton!" barked the whale rudely. "And I've had a bellyful of that on the way here!" She belched loudly.

"Of course, we'll stop the music—" Rani's grandmother tried again, but the whale interrupted her.

"You shouldn't have started it in the first place! I'm sick of you mermaids and your silly parties! You never think about anyone else but yourselves!" And she rammed her whole body against the side of the wreck again, in protest.

"The ceiling!" somebody yelled, as a

loud ripping noise came from above their heads and splinters of driftwood and barnacles started to fall from above.

The mermaids looked up and screamed. The huge wooden beams that made up the ceiling were splitting down the middle.

"What are we going to do?" gasped Flora, as everyone tried to swim away at once. "The roof garden will cave in on us."

Rani knew that there was no time to lose. She had to use the sea-spell. She took the golden shell from her belt and clasped it tightly in her hand, concentrating as hard as she could on starting up the magic. Gold dust began to trickle out from inside the shell – the spell was being released! Rani closed her eyes to help her focus better. When she opened them again, the water in the room was sparkling.

"What's happening?" someone cried out.

The whole room and its contents – except for the mermaids themselves – seemed to have frozen. A huge piece of ceiling had stopped in mid-water as it fell. A heavy rock from the roof garden, which had been about to fall on top of the band, was suspended in the water, not moving.

"Quick!" shouted Rani. "Everyone must swim out. Now!"

It took several minutes to clear the whole room so that only Rani was left.

A layer of sparkling water surrounded her as she closed her eyes again. Now, all she had to do was fix the ceiling and the roof garden would be saved. She remembered everything Morva had taught her and concentrated very hard on the spell.

Everyone cheered as the ceiling slipped back into place and the roof garden was restored.

Rani's grandmother leaned closer to Miriam as they waited for Rani to join them outside. She spoke very quietly so that no one else could hear. "I understand now what you mean about Rani," she whispered. "She is very special."

Miriam nodded. "I know."

"She may want to go and find her true home one day," the old mermaid added gently. "You realize that, don't you, my dear?"

Rani's mother didn't reply.

When she was sure that the spell had *really* worked, Rani swam outside to join the others. She knew that her mother and grandmother had been watching her very carefully, and now Miriam seemed quiet. "Mother, is something wrong?" she asked, swimming up to her. "You look sad."

"I'm fine, Rani," Miriam replied. "We all are . . . Thanks to you." And she pulled Rani close and gave her a very tight hug.

Suddenly, there was a big shout

behind them. It was Octavius, still clutching his bowl of trifle. "You mermaids really aren't very good at cooking," he muttered, fishing something hard and shiny out of it. And Rani saw that what Octavius was holding up – half covered in gooey trifle – was her amber pendant!

chapter Six

"Octopuses are very emotional, aren't they?" Kai said the following morning, as they waited for Octavius to finish saying goodbye to Flora. Having argued for most of the visit, the brother and sister were now embracing each other and getting horribly tangled up.

Rani had finally got the chance to speak to Flora on her own but she hadn't really discovered anything more about the mysterious red-haired mermaid. Flora was certain that her amber pendant had been the same kind as Rani's, though, and she had added that the young mermaid had been very sweet-natured. But apart from that Flora couldn't tell her anything else. She didn't know what had happened to the mermaid after she had left her – or to her baby.

Murdoch gently reminded everybody that they needed to set off.

"I can't wait to see Pearl again!" Kai said, as she waved goodbye to her grandmother.

"Me too," said Rani. "And Morva!" Rani was longing to tell Morva everything that had happened.

But the journey home seemed to take for ever. Roscoe was so tired that he kept falling asleep holding on to Miriam's hair.

"We're probably tired out from all that dancing," Murdoch said. "That's why it seems like it's taking longer. We'll stop and rest soon."

Rani turned to her mother and noticed something.

"Where's Roscoe?" she asked.

Roscoe was no longer attached to Miriam's hair – he had definitely been there the last time she'd looked – and he wasn't swimming along beside them either. In fact, he was nowhere in sight.

Everybody stopped swimming and started to call out Roscoe's name.

"He must have got lost," Murdoch said, frowning. "Come on. We'd better go back and look for him."

"I just hope he hasn't got himself eaten," Octavius said. "There was an extremely large fish back there. Did you see it?"

"Octavius, *please*," Miriam said.

"Sorry, sorry," muttered Octavius. "Of course, sea horses are very difficult to digest. That fish will probably just spit him straight out again if it's got any sense. Of course, fish *don't* have a lot of sense—"

"Octavius, *be quiet*!" Murdoch hissed. "I think I can hear something."

When the others listened they could hear the noise too. It sounded like someone shouting from a long way away.

"Come on," said Murdoch. "Stay

close to me."

They swam off in the direction of the sound. As they got nearer they could tell that it was definitely Roscoe.

"HELP!" Roscoe was shouting. "GET ME OUT OF HERE!"

"I hope he's not shouting from inside that fish's stomach," Octavius said gloomily.

"*OCTAVIUS!*" Miriam and Murdoch snapped at him together.

They swam on a little further and then they saw him.

"Oh no!" gasped Rani. The little sea horse was stuck in the middle of a gigantic silver web.

"Keep back, all of you!" Murdoch called out, sharply. "That's a Giant

Sea-Spider's web. That silver stuff is spider glue. If you touch it, you'll get stuck too."

"Father, what are we going to do?" Rani asked, starting to panic. Giant Sea-Spiders caught other creatures in their webs in order to eat them. Everyone knew that. And any spider with a web as big as this one had to have a very large appetite indeed.

"Find some rocks to throw at the web and we'll try to break it that way," Rani's father said. But he sounded very worried.

As the others began to collect rocks, Rani hovered beside the web. If only she hadn't used up the sea-spell. Surely there was *something* she could do. After all, she knew how to do a mending spell, didn't she? Surely a *breaking* spell couldn't be that different?

She closed her eyes and concentrated, holding out her hands so that they were just above the edge of the web. She focused as hard as she could on conjuring up a picture in her mind of the web breaking. Her belly button started to tingle and the tingling quickly spread up over the rest of her body and down her arms. Her fingertips felt hot. She opened her eyes and saw that golden sparks were jumping from her fingers to the web.

"Look at Rani!" Kai shouted.

For an instant the whole web sparkled. Then there was a sudden burst of golden

light, the web broke with a *ping* and
Roscoe was hurled straight into Rani's
arms.

"It's OK, Roscoe. You're safe now,"
Rani cried, hugging the trembling sea
horse.

The others were amazed. They knew
that Rani was learning to do magic but

none of them had ever seen her use it on her own before.

"You're just like Morva!" Kai stammered, looking at her sister in awe.

"Not quite," Rani laughed, pulling sticky bits of web out of her hair. "But I hope I will be, one day."

Just then, a large sea snake slithered over Rani's tail, followed by several babies. "Don't worry," the mother snake hissed. "We're not poisonous. But *she* is!" She flicked out her tongue to point at the huge, hairy, eight-legged creature crawling along the seabed towards them. "I'd get out of here if I was you!"

"SWIM!" commanded Murdoch, grabbing Kai and Rani and using his large, powerful tail to propel them at top speed through the water.

"Come back," shouted the sea-spider. "I won't eat you! I only put that web up because it looks pretty!"

"Do you think that's true?" Rani gasped, as they kept swimming.

"Somehow," Murdoch said, slowing down as they reached a safe distance away, "I didn't feel like taking her word for it."

"I have always thought that there is something quite *unnatural* about a creature with hairy legs," Octavius shuddered, waving his arms about in disgust.

"Come on," laughed Murdoch. "Let's go home."

Chapter Seven

Morva was trying to sing Pearl to sleep when they got home. She had tied some shells to some seaweed ribbons and made a beautiful shell-mobile which was dangling from the ceiling above Pearl's cradle. Pearl shrieked with excitement when she saw her parents and sisters again, and stretched out her chubby arms to be picked up by Miriam.

After everyone had hugged each other, Rani took Morva to one side.

"Morva, I've got so much to tell you!"

Rani began excitedly, but she stopped
when she saw the look on her friend's
face.

"Where did you get that?" Morva was
staring at the amber pendant around
Rani's neck as if she had just seen a
ghost.

"My grandmother gave it to me. It
was in her treasure chest. She gave a

necklace to Kai too. Look." She pointed to her sister who was swinging Pearl round and round, making her giggle. But Morva kept her eyes fixed on Rani.

"Rani, that is no ordinary stone—" Morva started to explain but, at that moment, Rani's mother called over to them.

"Morva, thank you so much for looking after Pearl. Would you like to stay and have supper with us?"

Morva shook her head, still looking dazed. "I must be getting back to my lobsters and my starfish. The poor things will be wondering where I am."

"But, Morva . . ." Rani began. "Tell me what's *wrong*."

"There's nothing *wrong*, Rani," Morva

said, as she swam towards the door.
"You've just given me a bit of a shock,
that's all. Come and see me tomorrow.
I'll explain everything then!"

As soon as she woke up the following
morning, Rani set off for Morva's cave.
Her mother made her have some
breakfast first, but she was too nervous to
eat more than a few mouthfuls.

Why had Morva looked so shocked
yesterday when she saw the pendant?
And what did she mean about it being
no ordinary stone?

When she arrived at the floating cave,
Morva was cooking breakfast on her hot-
rock stove. "So, Rani . . ." Morva turned
and smiled at her. "You have found your

message-stone. Or it has found you! It gave me quite a start yesterday, to see you with it." She swam over and touched Rani's amber pendant.

"*Message-stone?*" Rani frowned. She had never heard of such a thing.

Morva motioned for Rani to take off the necklace. As she took it from her, she said, "Look how it stops glowing when it leaves your skin. It is yours for certain!"

"Morva, what *is* a message-stone?" Rani demanded, getting impatient.

"A message-stone . . ." Morva explained slowly, "is a special stone that magic mermaids wear when they are separated from their families. That way they can always be sure that their loved ones are safe."

"I don't understand," Rani said. "How can a stone tell you that? And anyway, my family *is* safe. I've only just left them."

"I'm not talking about your family *here*," said Morva. "I mean your true family – the family you were separated from as a baby. If this is *your* message-stone . . . if you open it . . . you will see your true family inside."

"But how—" Rani gasped.

"A message-stone will always open for its true owner," Morva said, as she dropped it back into Rani's hand. "You must blow on it."

Rani lifted the amber stone up so that it was level with her face. She filled out her cheeks with air and blew.

"That's it," Morva said.

As they watched, the stone seemed to be glowing even brighter in Rani's hand. Gradually, its surface changed. Instead of being hard, it was becoming soft, like jelly.

"Look inside now," Morva urged her gently. "Go on. Don't be frightened."

Slowly, Rani lifted the stone up again and looked inside. It was like looking in through a window. Inside, she could see a merman, a mermaid and two babies. They all had red hair. The mermaid was young and beautiful and looked a bit like Rani. The merman was broad-shouldered and handsome.

"Is this . . . Are they . . . ?" Rani stammered, unable to say any more.

"This must be your family at the time you were separated from them," Morva whispered.

"But . . . but there are *two* babies!" Rani said hoarsely.

"I know. Watch carefully and see what happens next."

As she watched, Rani saw the two babies slowly changing before her eyes. "That's *me*," Rani gasped, as one of the babies grew into a little girl. At the same time, the other baby changed into a little boy with short red hair and twinkling goldy-brown eyes like Rani's.

"You must have a twin brother," Morva said.

Only the man and the woman didn't change. As Rani watched, they slowly faded away until they had completely disappeared.

"Where have they gone? What does it mean?" Rani cried out.

"It means," explained Morva gently, "that your real parents must have died when you were a baby. I'm sorry, Rani."

Rani swallowed. She had known for a long time that her true parents might be dead. But somehow actually *seeing* them and then watching them disappear like that made the fact that they were gone for ever seem a lot more real. She would never meet them now. She felt a tear roll down her cheek.

"Did you know them?" she asked Morva.

"I didn't recognize them, no," Morva

said. "But remember how old I am,
Rani. I left my home a long, long time
before you were born . . . probably
before your parents were born too."

Rani was silent.

"Your brother is still alive though,"
Morva added, trying to cheer her up.
"Imagine that! A twin brother!"

"He probably doesn't even know he

has a sister," said Rani sadly.

Morva smiled. "I wouldn't be so sure. How do you know that he hasn't got his own message-stone, with *you* inside it?"

"Do you really think so?" That thought made Rani feel better. She looked up at Morva. "I want you to take me to the place *you* come from – the magic place – so that I can find him."

"I *will* take you," Morva said. "But you must be patient, Rani. Your magic is not yet strong enough for you to make the journey."

"When will it be strong enough?" Rani demanded impatiently.

"Soon," Morva replied, smiling. "Very soon – I promise! And until then you can watch your brother growing up inside

your pendant. Now, come on. It's time
we practised another spell. How about
I teach you how to turn my breakfast
into enough to eat for two?"

Rani laughed. She had to admit that
she *was* starting to feel a bit hungry.

Chapter Eight

The next day Octavius invited them all round for supper.

"What do you think of our new necklaces?" Kai asked Morva, who was looking especially colourful in a red and orange seaweed shawl.

"Very pretty indeed," Morva replied. Both Morva and Rani had thought it best if no one else knew about the message-stone yet, so they had agreed to keep it as a secret between the two of them.

Octavius had cooked his best stew and everyone complimented him on how delicious it was as they tucked in and listened to him telling Morva the story of the huge whale. "Of course, I warned everyone about that ceiling before the party started," he reminded them, not

for the first time. "I don't like to say 'I told you so' but really . . . If you mermaids would only listen to me instead of—"

Morva interrupted him. "I hear your *stew* saved the day as well, Octavius," she said, giving Rani a wink. "Tell us about that!"

"My stew? Ah, yes, my stew . . . It's a good job I had the idea of throwing that shark my stew," Octavius said. "Otherwise I don't know what would have become of us all."

"But it was *Rani* who told you to throw the stew," Kai pointed out.

"Rani? Ah, yes – Rani had the same idea as me," Octavius blustered. "I remember we both had the idea at the same time. Well done, Rani!"

"I'm just glad you brought that stew with you, Octavius," Rani said quickly. "Or I don't know what we'd have done." She turned to Morva. "I dropped the sea-spell, you see, so we couldn't use that."

"Well, it sounds as if you put my sea-spell to very good use in the end, Rani," Morva replied. "And then used some magic of your own on the journey home, I hear!"

"She saved my life!" Roscoe butted in. "If it wasn't for Rani—"

". . . you'd be digested by now!" Octavius finished for him.

The little sea horse shuddered.

"Let's make a toast," said Murdoch,

holding up his glass of mer-wine. "To Rani – our very own magic mermaid!"

"And the best sister anyone could have!" added Kai, grinning.

"So are you!" replied Rani, swimming over to give her sister a hug. "And you, Pearl!" she added, quickly kissing her baby sister who was sitting on Kai's lap.

"Rani *also* has the most beautiful singing voice," Octavius told Morva. "I was hoping that she would sing for us tonight."

"I don't *really* have a beautiful voice," Rani murmured, touching her pendant.

"What do you mean?" Morva asked.

"Rani reckons she can't sing unless she's wearing her amber pendant," Kai said. "That's what you said at the party, isn't it, Rani?"

"Well, that's just silly," Rani's parents exclaimed at once. "Whatever gave you that idea, Rani?"

"Well . . ." Rani began, wondering if she ought to explain after all about the pendant being magic, but Morva interrupted her.

"You know, I've seen you become a lot more confident lately, Rani," she said, thoughtfully. "Perhaps that's what's made the difference."

"Do you really think so?" asked Rani doubtfully.

"There's only one way to find out," Morva replied. "Give me the pendant."

Rani handed it to her.

"Now," Morva said, "*I'll* hold the pendant while *you* sing."

Rani stared at her in horror. "*No way!*"

"Come on, Rani," Morva said. "You couldn't have been that bad at singing before!"

"I sounded all croaky like a sea-frog," Rani replied.

Everyone laughed.

When the laughter had died down, Octavius cleared his throat loudly. "Of course, *I* could always sing if Rani doesn't want to. I'm told I have rather a splendid voice myself."

The others looked at each other in alarm.

"Why don't we *all* sing?" suggested Morva quickly.

So that's what they did. And as they sang, Rani heard her own voice, rising confident and clear above the others, and that was when she noticed that Morva was still holding her pendant.

Morva swam over to her. "Magic isn't the answer to everything, Rani," she whispered. "Don't ever forget that!"

And Rani promised that she wouldn't

as Morva dropped the message-stone, with her brother inside, back around her neck.

The
Shell
Princess

In memory of my father and grandfather

Chapter One

Rani's long red hair streamed out behind her as she swam through the clear, warm water of Tingle Reef. She was going to visit her friend, Morva, who lived in a floating cave on the edge of the reef. To get there you had to swim past a sea-cactus with blue flowers and then carry on until you came to a needle-shaped bush which pointed up towards the magic rock where Morva lived.

Morva was a magic mermaid, just like Rani. Both of them had orange tails and

long red hair, unlike the other mermaids who had blonde hair and green tails. Morva had been teaching Rani how to use her special powers ever since Rani had discovered that she could do magic too.

As she entered Morva's cave, Rani stopped to stare at the painting on the wall. It showed a red-haired mermaid swimming down through what looked like a giant burst of golden light.

"You look thoughtful," said Morva, swimming up behind her.

"I was just wondering," Rani said, "if you ever miss your old home."

Although Morva had lived in Tingle Reef for a very long time, she had not been born there. She had grown up in a secret place, far away in the Deep Blue, where magic mermaids lived. The giant golden light in the picture was the entrance to the magic mermaids' home.

"Sometimes I do," Morva said. "Sometimes I dream about it."

"I wish I could remember it," sighed Rani.

Rani had been found in Tingle Reef

as a baby – inside a Giant Clam-Shell – and she had lived there ever since. She had been adopted by a family who she loved very much, but she had always felt curious about the place she had really come from.

"That mermaid looks *so* beautiful," Rani said, still gazing at the picture. "I hope I look like her when I grow up."

"Perhaps you'll look like me," Morva teased.

"Oh, no!" said Rani at once. "I could never look as beautiful as you!"

Morva's red hair stretched to the tip of her tail and shone so brightly that Morva could always be spotted in dark water from a long way away. Not that the water in Tingle Reef was ever dark – it

was a lovely clear blue colour which
made the reef such a wonderful place to
live. But Rani had made a few trips with
Morva into the Deep Blue, and she had
noticed that the darker the water
became, the more Morva's hair seemed
to glow.

"Just like my pendant," Rani thought,
looking down at it. Rani's amber
pendant was a gift from her
grandmother, and it seemed to glow
against Rani's skin. It wasn't just any
necklace – it was a message-stone. *Her*
message-stone. Magic mermaids use
message-stones to see their families when
they became separated from them. Rani
had learned by looking into her message-
stone that her true parents had died

when she was a baby, but that she had a twin brother. When she looked in her message-stone and saw his red hair and twinkly eyes looking back at her, she could hardly wait to meet him.

"Morva, *when* will you take me there?" Rani asked, gazing longingly at the painting.

"I told you, Rani," Morva replied. "When your magic is stronger."

"But my magic is strong now," Rani protested. "I've been practising really hard. Look!" And she closed her eyes and concentrated on turning the water in Morva's cave from crystal clear to bright pink. When she opened her eyes the water was orange.

"Oh dear," Morva laughed, quickly

turning it back again.

Rani felt silly and feeling silly made her cross. "It's not fair!" she said, banging the end of her tail impatiently against the floor of the cave. "*Why* do I have to keep waiting?"

Morva stopped laughing. Rani was usually very good-tempered. "I didn't

realize it was upsetting you so much, Rani," she said gently. "I know how hard you've been practising your magic and it's getting stronger all the time. But I didn't think there was any need to rush. I thought you were happy here in Tingle Reef."

"I *am* happy here," replied Rani. "But I really want to meet *him*!" She held the pendant in her hands and looked inside at the face of her brother. "He misses me just as much, I know he does. I have to find him!"

"Listen carefully, Rani," Morva said, looking at her gravely. "The first thing you have to realize is that your brother may not be where we think he is. If your parents put you inside a Giant

Clam-Shell in order to keep you safe, they probably did the same with your brother. He might not have been found by his own people. Like you, he may have been adopted by a different group of mermaids, and if so he could be anywhere."

Rani shook her head. "Morva, I just know he got back safely," she said. "I can *feel* it."

Morva paused, as if she was thinking really hard about something. "There's something else you should know," she said. "Another reason you might not be ready to make the journey back yet." She swam over to the painting and placed her hand over the place where the golden light seemed to be rising out

of the seabed. "Watch carefully," she
commanded.

As Rani watched, a gold line started to
appear all by itself, on top of the picture.
"What is it?" she gasped.

"Look more carefully," Morva told
her, as the line spread.

Rani swam back to look at the gold

lines from a greater distance, and then she knew. "It's a map!" she said. "A golden map."

"That's right," Morva nodded. "This map shows us the way home."

She lifted her hand from the wall and the lines instantly disappeared.

"Bring it back!" gasped Rani. "We need it to find our way there."

"I remember the way quite clearly. I don't need a map," Morva replied. "But the map has another purpose."

Rani frowned. "What do you mean?"

"Any mermaid can follow a map and swim across the Deep Blue," Morva said. "But only a magic mermaid can swim through the golden light to get to our home. And if a mermaid can make the map appear, then it means her magic power is strong enough to let her in."

"Please, can I try?" asked Rani excitedly.

"The magic in the hand that touches the picture must be very strong in order for the map to show itself," Morva warned her. "If you try too soon, you may be disappointed."

"I still want to see if I can do it," Rani said.

"Very well," Morva said, moving back from the wall. "If you *really* want to put your magic to the test . . ."

Chapter Two

Slowly, Rani placed her hand flat against the picture on Morva's wall. Nothing happened at first, then she felt her hand starting to tingle.

"Look," she whispered, holding in her breath as gold lines began to appear on the cave wall. "I've done it!"

Morva nodded slowly.

"So my magic *is* strong enough!" Rani said, turning her head to look at Morva. "Does that mean I'm ready to visit my brother?"

"In a way, yes," Morva replied carefully. "But there are different ways of being ready, Rani. Are you sure you're ready to leave your family? And are *they* ready for you to go?"

Rani frowned. The truth was that she hadn't told her family anything about this yet.

"I'm sure they'll let me," she said. "I'll go and ask them now!"

But as she swam back towards her own cave, she started to worry. What if her family were against the idea? Her parents could be so protective of her sometimes, especially her mother. She couldn't just leave Tingle Reef without telling them. She loved them too much to do that. She sighed. She would just

have to *make* them see how important
it was for her to make this trip, that
was all!

When Rani got back home to their
cave, her mother, Miriam, was cooking
dinner while her father, Murdoch,
bounced her baby sister, Pearl, on the
end of his tail. Rani's other sister, Kai,
was peering into the cooking pot and
complaining that they were having
seaweed *again*. "Mother, Father, Kai . . .
I've got something to tell you," Rani
began.

But before she could continue, there
was a knock on the wall outside and four
long wriggly arms pushed back their
seaweed-flap.

"Good day, everyone," said Octavius

the octopus, as he peered in through one of the gaps he had made in the seaweed curtain. "May I come in?"

"Of course," said Murdoch. "Though we're just about to have dinner."

Rani noticed that her mother was frowning. Octavius had a habit of visiting at inconvenient times and staying for ages.

"I've already had my dinner," Octavius said, settling himself on the most comfortable rock. "Some of my delicious stew. Do you know, I don't believe I've ever tasted anything as fine as my very own cooking? I don't know why I should be such a talented cook – unless it's another consequence of having such a large brain. I suppose I *am* able to put a lot of thought into my recipes."

Rani felt impatient. Once Octavius got started on the subject of his brain, he was impossible to stop. She would never get to speak to her family at this rate. Then she had an idea. As Octavius continued to boast, Rani decided to try out some magic. As she focused on him she could feel her magic struggling against a very strong force indeed. She concentrated extra-hard, and was beginning to feel a bit dizzy, when something weird started to happen. Golden sparks appeared around Octavius's mouth as he said, "Of course, my brain is really just of average size for an octopus."

Miriam and Murdoch stared at him in disbelief and Kai nearly dropped the shell-cutlery she was putting on the table.

"And in any case," continued Octavius, "quantity does not always mean quality." And he gave them a humble smile as he exited their cave.

"I don't believe it!" gasped Miriam.

They all started to laugh.

Rani decided that now was as good a time as any to break her news. "Mother, Father, Kai . . ." she began again firmly, and this time they all turned to listen.

"A magic stone?" frowned Miriam, when Rani had finished. "I don't understand."

"It's a *message*-stone, Mother," Rani said. "Morva showed me how to open the pendant and we found out that my real parents must have died when I was a baby. They were in some sort of danger and that was why they put me inside the Clam-Shell. But I had a twin brother and they put him inside another shell or something because he's still alive."

Rani's mother sat on the seaweed mat, looking dazed. "And now you want to leave us in order to find him?"

"I don't *want* to leave you," Rani said, "but I have to find my brother. You can't come with me because only magic mermaids can go to the place Morva comes from."

"It sounds far too dangerous," Miriam said. "And you are too young to make such a big journey. Perhaps when you're older—"

"It's not dangerous!" Rani protested. "Morva will be with me. Please, Mother, I'm ready to go *now*!"

But her mother was shaking her head firmly.

Rani looked at her father. Surely Murdoch would understand. "Father?" she pleaded. "Please say I can go!"

"We think of you as belonging here with us, Rani," Murdoch said gently, "that's the problem." He sighed. "I'm afraid I agree with your mother. I don't want you to go either. You don't know what you will find there, Rani. It may not make you happy. And we don't want to lose you."

"You won't lose me," Rani said, fighting back tears. Why couldn't they understand? They *had* to let her go! Otherwise *she* was going to lose her brother!

Chapter Three

Rani's pet sea horse, Roscoe, was swinging himself on one of the seaweed swings in the shell-garden. He looked a bit huffy when Rani approached and flipped himself round on the swing so that he had his back to her.

Rani realized that she hadn't spent much time with Roscoe recently – she'd been too busy practising her magic.

"I'm sorry, Roscoe," Rani said, stroking his bony head. "I haven't been a very good friend lately – have I?"

"No, you haven't," Roscoe said crossly.
But he couldn't help smiling when Rani
tickled his neck. He turned around and
listened as Rani explained what had just
happened.

"So . . ." said Roscoe, when she had
finished. "You don't want to lose *this*
family but you can't bear not to find your

other family as well. That seems fair enough to me!"

"Try telling that to Mother and Father," Rani sighed.

Roscoe looked thoughtful. "We need to think of a way of making them see this from your point of view," he said.

"Yes, but how?" Rani asked him.

Roscoe thought about it. "I know! Who has more clever thoughts in one day than you mermaids have in a whole year?"

"Octavius," Rani replied. "At least, that's what he's always *saying*, but—"

"Exactly. *This* is his chance to prove his point," Roscoe interrupted her. "We'll tell him the problem and he'll *have* to come up with an idea just to prove to us how clever he is!"

"But what if it isn't a *good* idea?" Rani asked nervously.

"So?" Roscoe said, flicking her with his tail as he jumped off the swing. "Do you have *any* ideas *at all*?"

Rani shook her head.

"Well, come on, then!" And the little sea horse bobbed ahead of her towards Octavius's cave.

As soon as Roscoe tapped his bony tail against the cave wall to be let in, the octopus yelled at them to go away. "You know I always rest my brain at this time of the day!" he shouted.

Rani sighed. Still, at least that meant that Octavius had returned to his usual self.

"Octavius, this is an emergency!" shouted the sea horse. "Rani needs your help."

"Rani?" Octavius grumbled as he swam over to his seaweed-flap and lifted it up. "Can't she use her magic to sort it out, whatever it is? I'm really very tired."

"This isn't a problem for magic," Roscoe continued perkily. "This is a problem that can only be solved by some clever *thinking*."

"Well, really," grunted the octopus.

"*Very* clever thinking, Octavius," Roscoe repeated, and paused dramatically. "That's why we've come to you."

"I see. Hmm," Octavius looked flustered. "Well, I suppose you'd better come in and tell me what the problem is. I'll certainly have some clever thoughts about it – but my clever thoughts can sometimes be *too* clever to actually put into action, you understand." He coughed.

"Octavius, I don't know what to do . . ." Rani began to explain her problems.

As Octavius listened, his big forehead formed a very crinkly brow.

"I've got to persuade Mother and Father to let me go, or I'll never get to meet my brother," Rani finished, starting to cry.

"Oh dear, oh dear," muttered Octavius, who was really very soft-hearted when it came to mermaids

crying. He placed all his arms round
Rani in a very complicated hug.

"You look like you're trapped inside a
cage of octopus-arms," Roscoe joked,
trying to cheer her up.

And it was then that it happened.
Octavius grunted out loud as the idea hit
him. It was a very clever idea – the

cleverest he'd ever had!

"Leave it to me," he told Rani, extracting his arms one by one. "You go back home and wait for me. I won't be long. I just have to make something first."

And he dashed outside his cave, churning up the water in his hurry.

Later on that day, Rani's family were sitting quietly in their cave. Things had felt very tense when Rani returned although no one had said any more about her request to leave Tingle Reef. It seemed that as far as her parents were concerned, the matter was closed. Kai was hardly speaking to her, though, and even Pearl seemed to sense that something was wrong, refusing to settle down to sleep even with Rani's mother singing to her.

Pearl had just about dropped off when Octavius arrived. He was carrying a strange contraption which he set down proudly on the floor of the cave.

"I have to show you this," he said. "It's a special cage. I made it out of razor shells and spider-glue – and the mesh is made out of bind-weed. A very clever invention, don't you think?"

"What's it for?" Miriam asked.

"I'm going to use it to catch a magic fish!" Octavius said. "They live way out in the Deep Blue and are said to be very beautiful indeed. A whole shoal of them is coming to visit Morva tomorrow."

"But, Octavius, you can't trap a magic fish here," Miriam protested. "It wouldn't be fair."

"Why not? I really want one for a pet. You have Roscoe, don't you?"

"That's different," said Murdoch. "Roscoe *chooses* to live with us. You can't keep a magic fish here against its will."

"Hmm," said Octavius, pretending to

think about it. "What do you think, Rani?"

Before she could reply, Miriam turned on Octavius, her eyes flashing angrily. "Is this your clumsy way of telling us that you think we should let Rani go with Morva?"

Octavius turned a bit pink. "Well, she did come to me in great distress and I do think—"

Miriam turned away from him to face Rani. "You went to Octavius to ask for help?"

Rani nodded. "But, Mother—"

"Well, all I can say, Rani," Miriam interrupted her crisply, "is that in that case you must have felt pretty desperate!"

"I beg your pardon—" began Octavius huffily.

"She didn't mean it like that, Octavius," Murdoch hastily intervened. "We're just shocked that Rani feels so strongly about this that she chose to go to someone outside the family about it, that's all." He paused.

There was an awkward silence.

Finally Rani's mother spoke. "I don't ever want your home to feel like a prison to you, Rani," she said, staring at Octavius's cage. "If you need to find this other place so badly – and if Morva will be there to look after you – then . . ." – she looked at her husband to check that he agreed – ". . . Then perhaps we should think about letting you go."

"Oh, Mother, thank you!" gasped Rani, rushing to give her a hug.

"But *if* we let you go with Morva, you must promise to come back to us!" Miriam added sharply.

"Of course I'll come back," laughed Rani. She turned to her sister. "Kai – no other sister could ever be as good as you! When I find my brother, I know he'll want you to be *his* sister too!"

"Oh, dear me," said Octavius, dabbing at his eyes with an old piece of seaweed. Mermaids were so *emotional*! Honestly, if it wasn't for him and his clever thinking, then goodness knows *what* would become of them all!

Chapter Four

Rani couldn't believe she was really going with Morva.

Morva was excited too when she came to collect her. "I can't wait to see my old home again!" she beamed.

Rani and her family took ages saying goodbye, so that Morva began to wonder if they were ever going to leave at all, but eventually, after a final round of hugs, the two mermaids set off.

"We are going further away than you could possibly imagine, Rani," Morva told her, when they were finally out of sight of Tingle Reef. "This is like no other journey you have ever made before. We will be travelling further into the Deep Blue than any Tingle Reef mermaid has *ever* travelled." She paused. "First, though, we have to swim a lot faster. I believe it's time to use some magic!"

And all that anyone watching would have seen after that, were two streaks of gold light speeding through the water.

"This is where we catch our whale," Morva said, finally stopping at a very unusual-looking rock with several mermaid-sized seats chiselled out of it. "This is a whale-stop. We must sit and wait."

"A *whale-stop*?" Rani repeated, in disbelief.

"That's right. I'm not talking about your average whale. I'm talking about the Giant Whales who live out in the Deep Blue," Morva explained. "They have always been friends to us magic mermaids."

Morva started to make some strange whale-calling noises, and soon two huge white eyes appeared next to the rock, making Rani jump. The sea was so dark that it was hard to see the rest of the creature's body.

Morva reached out and patted the whale's nose, which was the same size as her hand. "Did you have trouble finding us? My whale-calls are a bit

rusty, I'm afraid."

The whale told them that his name was Jonah and that he had seen their hair shining from a long way away. Rani saw that his head was so huge that, if he opened his mouth, he could easily have devoured them both in one bite. "Where are you going?" he asked. "Home?"

Morva nodded. "Have you room for two of us?"

"I expect so – if you're careful. Swim inside."

"Thank you. Come on, Rani," Morva said, easing herself off the rock.

"Swim inside *what*?" asked Rani.

"Why, inside Jonah's mouth, of course. Look – he's opened it for us." Morva swam in and beckoned for Rani to follow. "Come on, Rani. You know very well that whales only eat plankton."

Rani still felt a bit unsure as she slowly swam in between the whale's huge jaws to join her friend. Rani saw that the whale didn't have any teeth but had a bony sieve inside its mouth which it used to sift out plankton from the water.

"Now," said Morva. "You must keep very still – no splashing around or he'll get cross with us."

"I'll keep *very* still," Rani promised, not relishing the idea of Jonah getting cross with her while she was sitting inside his mouth.

Rani soon discovered that there was nothing to be alarmed about. The whale's mouth was soft and warm, and the journey from then on was quite comfortable. His mouth was shut so they couldn't see where they were going but that didn't seem to worry Morva.

Soon Rani fell asleep and started to dream that she was back in Tingle Reef with all her family – but her brother was there too. It was such a happy dream that she didn't want to wake up when Morva finally shook her gently and told her that they had to get out.

"Why? Are we there already?" Rani asked, thinking that perhaps she had been asleep for longer than she'd thought.

"No, but Jonah has stopped. There's some sort of problem. Now, stay close to me, Rani. This part of the Deep Blue is very dark and it's very easy to get lost."

As they swam out of Jonah's mouth, Rani shivered because the water here was so cold.

"What's wrong?" Morva asked the whale.

Jonah told them to swim underneath his belly and look down.

They swam under and saw that they were very close to the seabed.

"It's a shark!" Rani gasped, pointing below them to a long black fish with a huge pointed nose and sharp white teeth. The shark was nudging something that looked like a white furry ball.

"What's it got?" Rani whispered, starting to swim closer.

Morva pulled her back. "Be careful.

We don't want it to see us."

The white ball – whatever it was – was making sobbing noises. Suddenly a little black nose became visible, then two blue eyes and two little white ears.

"I don't believe it," Morva gasped. "It's a bear cub!"

"A *bear cub*!" Rani repeated. She had heard stories about the Great White Swimming Bears that lived on the other side of the Deep Blue but she had never seen one before. "What's it doing here?"

"That shark must have caught it," Morva said.

At that moment three more sharks appeared – another adult one and two youngsters. "Dad, what's for dinner?" one of the young ones demanded.

"We're starving!"

"This," the biggest shark replied, prodding the whimpering bear cub. "And we have to eat it straight away before its mother comes looking for it."

"Morva – we've got to *do* something!" gasped Rani, as the little bear looked towards them helplessly.

"Do you remember that tasting spell I taught you?" Morva whispered. "The one that you tried on Kai, that made her think seaweed tasted delicious?"

Rani nodded. How could she ever forget the day Kai had asked for a second helping of greens? "But how will that help?"

"I'll do it in reverse," Morva said. "Watch." And as Morva closed her eyes and concentrated, Rani saw little gold sparks beginning to appear around the mouth of the biggest shark as he sank his teeth into the bear cub's white fur.

The shark let out a snort of disgust and dropped the little bear before he had even taken a bite. "Yuck!" he said, spitting out a bit of fur. "That tastes horrible."

The other sharks were frowning. Baby bear was normally delicious.

Just then an angry roar sounded from above.

"MUMMY!" shouted the little bear cub. "I'm down here!"

A furious mother bear came charging down through the water, her white fur standing on end as she growled in rage.

She lashed out with her sharp claws at
the sharks, who quickly panicked and
swam off.

Rani waved as she and Morva
watched the mother bear and her cub
paddle away. The little bear kept turning
back to look at the two mermaids, as if
he couldn't believe his eyes.

"Where do swimming bears live?" Rani asked.

"Nobody knows for certain," Morva said, leading the way back to where Jonah was waiting for them. "Except that to get there you have to keep swimming up until you can't swim any further. Mermaids get dizzy if they swim that high, which is why nobody's ever been there."

"Now, Rani," Morva said, when they were safely back inside Jonah's warm mouth. "I want you to try and get some rest now."

Rani soon fell asleep and this time she dreamed she was swimming in sparkling water where big furry white bears swam along lazily beside her.

chapter five

"Wake up, Rani," Morva said, poking her. "We're here."

"*Where?*" Rani asked dozily, and then she remembered. She was about to meet her brother. And not just in a dream!

As Jonah opened his mouth for them to swim out, she blinked because the sea outside was full of a bright light. "It looks like . . . It looks like . . ." she gasped, but she couldn't continue because she had never seen anything like this before.

They were right on the sea-bottom and in front of them there seemed to be an opening in the seabed, from which a gold surge of light rose upwards through the water. The water all around glowed and Rani held up her arms to shield her eyes from the glare.

"Don't cover your eyes, Rani," Morva

told her. "You must look into the brightness. It won't hurt you."

Slowly, Rani looked. Her eyes seemed to be getting used to the bright water and she started to feel a strong tingling sensation in her skin.

"You've been wonderful, Jonah!" Morva said, swimming up to kiss him on the nose. Rani felt too shy to give him a kiss so she thanked him and gave him a pat instead.

As Jonah swam upwards and disappeared, Morva took hold of Rani's hand. "Your magic normally starts from inside you, Rani," she explained. "That's why you feel it in your belly button first. But now the magic is all around you. How do you feel?"

"I feel . . . strange," Rani said.

Morva smiled. "Now comes the strangest bit of all. We must swim down through that golden beam into that hole in the seabed."

"B-but . . ." Rani stammered. "There is nothing under the seabed." She had always been taught that the seabed was where everything ended.

"If you are a magic mermaid, it is different," Morva said gently. "Come with me."

And together they swam right into the beam of golden light. Rani felt warm inside and out. The tingling she usually felt in her fingers when she did magic felt as though it had taken over her whole body. She tried to speak but found that no words came.

"*Think* your thoughts to me, Rani," Rani could hear Morva saying inside her head. Thought-reading was part of her magic. "We will be able to speak to each other again when we have passed through the magic light."

The light was so strong that Rani could hardly see Morva as they swam downwards. As the brightness gradually lessened, Rani saw that she was swimming through a golden passageway under the seabed. "Wow!" she gasped.

"I know," said Morva, speaking out loud again. "I had forgotten how beautiful it was."

"But where does it lead to?" Rani asked.

"Wait and see," Morva smiled.

Eventually the passageway opened out into a huge cave. The cave was empty but the walls were decorated with pictures of mermaids swimming – all of them with red hair. They could hear voices now.

"This way," said Morva, and she swam over to an arched opening in the cave wall. "Through here," she said, swimming through and disappearing.

For a moment Rani felt nervous. Then she too swam through the archway and found herself in the most beautiful garden she could ever have dreamed of.

She had never seen flowers like these before – as tall as mermaids, with huge petals of bright colours. Huge oyster shells lazed about, proudly displaying their pearls for everyone to see, and beautiful golden fish swam between the feathery plants, playing hide and seek with each other. But what Rani couldn't stop staring at were the mermaids themselves. They all had orange tails – some tipped with gold – and every one of them had red hair like Rani's.

A young mermaid swam over, looking at them curiously. "Who are you?" she asked.

"I am Morva," Morva told her, looking as if she expected this to make some sort of impression, which it obviously did not.

"I'm Rani," Rani added quickly. "We're from Tingle Reef."

"Where's that?" asked the mermaid.

"A very long way away from here," Morva said, staring round at the other mermaids to see if she recognized any of them. "Perhaps you can help us. I need to speak to an *old* person – a *very* old person, you understand."

The young mermaid peered into Morva's eyes as if she had only just noticed that Morva was a lot older than she had first thought. "I'll take you to the Mer-King," she said. "He's *ancient!*"

"That will do very nicely," Morva said smiling.

Rani kept a sharp look-out for her brother as she followed closely behind her friend. They were led into another passageway and through into another cave and out again into a large courtyard.

"The Mer-King's palace is that way," the mermaid said, pointing to a pathway of golden shells. "Just follow those."

Rani and Morva thanked her and swam along until the shells came to an end a short distance away from the entrance to a very grand cave. Two rock pillars had been erected outside the arched cave-opening and a merman with a smart seaweed belt stood guard outside.

"Come on," whispered Morva. "Let's see if the Mer-King knows your brother."

And trembling a little, Rani waited as Morva swam forward and requested permission to be let inside.

Chapter Six

After the guard had sent a messenger inside the palace, Morva came back to wait with Rani.

"What if the Mer-King won't see us?" Rani asked, trying not to flick up any of the golden shells accidentally with her tail.

"Oh, he'll see us," Morva said confidently.

And at that moment, an old merman appeared, staring at them from the palace entrance. His red hair was streaked with white and he had a gold seaweed crown on his head. "Someone said that Morva was here!" he boomed out.

Morva swam forward, smiling. "She is."

The Mer-King stared into her eyes in disbelief. "*Morva!*" he exclaimed. "After all these years!" And he grabbed her hand and squeezed it excitedly. "Nobody knew what became of you! Come in! Come in! You must tell me everything!"

"Wait," said Morva, motioning for Rani to come forward. "I have brought someone with me. This is my friend Rani."

"You are very welcome, Rani," the Mer-King beamed at her. "Now you

must both come inside." And he led the way back into the palace.

"You *know* him?" Rani hissed to Morva, under her breath, as they followed him past the two massive pillars.

"Oh yes," smiled Morva. "We were great friends!"

"I was a very handsome Mer-Prince in those days, Rani," the Mer-King said, turning round to wink at her. "Can you imagine that?"

"Well . . ." Rani said, blushing, and the king laughed.

The palace was made out of many interconnecting caves, none of which seemed all that grand, until the king led them through a small archway into his main chamber. A carpet of gold moss covered the floor and the walls were a sparkly blue that reminded Rani of the water in Tingle Reef. Gold and silver fish of all sizes swam around inside the room and gold seaweed was strung from the ceiling. In the centre of the room, a silver dish was piled high with the most delicious-looking sea-fruits imaginable.

There were several soft seaweed cushions scattered about the floor, and the Mer-King flopped down on one and stretched out his tail with a sigh. "Sit down, sit down!" he urged them. "The Mer-Queen is out at the moment but she will be back soon. You must dine with us. You must be hungry after your long journey."

He snapped his fingers and ordered

some refreshments while they waited.

"Who did you marry?" Morva asked him. "No – let me guess!" And she reeled off a whole list of names that meant absolutely nothing to Rani. Morva began to ask about each of her old friends in turn, until Rani grew quite bored. If only there was somebody here to play with! Rani's ears pricked up as she heard Morva ask, "Do you have any children?"

The Mer-King looked sad. "We had a son – but he died a long time ago in a sea-quake." He quickly attempted to smile. "But this is a happy day! Let us not talk of sad things."

Rani was longing to ask the Mer-King if he knew her brother but Morva was asking so many questions that she couldn't get a word in.

Morva started to tell the Mer-King about Tingle Reef and about Rani turning up as a baby inside a Giant Clam-Shell. "Nobody knew that she was a magic mermaid, except me," said Morva. "And I have always promised her that one day I would bring her here." Morva leaned over and touched Rani's amber pendant. "We didn't know anything about her true family at all – until we found this."

"A message-stone," the Mer-King said, looking at Rani more closely.

"Yes – and inside Rani found a picture of her parents and learned that they had died when she was a baby. But there was another baby inside the stone – a boy who we know is the same age now as Rani. So I have explained to Rani that she must have a twin brother . . ." Morva paused. "And we were hoping that he might be here."

The Mer-King was staring intently at Rani now. "May I see the picture of this boy?" he asked.

Rani removed the stone from her neck and gently blew on it. As they watched, the surface softened and her brother's face appeared, looking out at her from inside.

The Mer-King looked over her shoulder at the face of the boy and gasped, "I don't believe it!"

"Do you know him?" asked Morva.

"This is my grandson," the Mer-King
said, putting a hand on Rani's shoulder
and turning her to face him.

Rani felt her heart start to beat faster.
If this was true . . . If her twin brother
was really the Mer-King's grandson,
then that meant . . .

The Mer-King was looking at her with
tears in his eyes now. "I-I can't believe

it," he stammered, as he touched her with a trembling hand. "Rani – you must be the lost Shell Princess!"

Rani and Morva listened as the Mer-King told them how his son and his son's young wife had been on a trip in the Deep Blue when they had sent a message saying that they would have to delay their return home because their baby was about to arrive.

"We went to find them," the Mer-King said, "but by the time we got there, a terrible sea-quake had destroyed the whole of the seabed where they were. We thought they had all been killed until we came across a Giant Clam-Shell. My grandson was inside. He was just a few days old. They must have put him inside the shell to protect him. He had a message-stone round his neck – just like yours, Rani. We couldn't look inside the stone until he was old enough to open it for us. When he told us he could see a little girl smiling at him, we thought he was making it up. But then we looked and, sure enough, there was this little red-haired mer-girl smiling out at us, with a face exactly like her mother's. We searched everywhere we could think of. We searched for years. But in the end we were forced to stop looking . . ."

The Mer-King touched Rani's hair. "I should have recognized you straight away," he told her. "But I have not looked at your picture for a very long time. It upset me to be reminded that my little granddaughter was out there somewhere all alone."

"Oh, but I wasn't alone—" Rani started to tell him, but she was interrupted by the palace messenger.

"The Mer-Queen and the Mer-Prince have returned," he announced.

At that moment an excited voice shouted, "Grandfather!" and a boy of Rani's age, with short red hair and sparkling eyes, came swimming into the room. "Guess what—" He stopped short when he saw Rani and Morva.

"Let me introduce my grandson," the Mer-King said. "Rani, this is Peri."

"Hello," the boy said, looking a bit dazed as he slowly took in Rani's face, her hair and, finally, her amber pendant.

Rani swallowed. She found that she couldn't speak properly. "I'm-I'm . . ." she stammered.

Peri flipped his tail in excitement. "I know who you are! You're the girl in my pendant!" And he dived forward and grabbed Rani by the hands. "You're my *sister*, aren't you?"

Rani nodded as Peri started to spin her non-stop around the room.

"Peri, calm down!" his grandfather called out. "You'll make Rani dizzy."

"It's OK!" Rani laughed, looking lovingly into her brother's eyes. "I don't mind!"

And Rani knew that she wouldn't be able to stop feeling giddy today, even if she tried.

Chapter Seven

Rani and Peri spent the next few days getting to know each other. The longer they spent together, the more they liked each other, and soon they felt that they had never been separated at all.

"It helped being able to see you inside my message-stone," Peri told her. "I used to talk to you all the time so it was sort of like having you with me. But it's much better now because you can talk back!"

Rani laughed. "Ever since I first saw you inside *my* message-stone, I've been longing to meet you! I can't believe I'm really here with you. I keep thinking I must be dreaming and that I'll wake up and find myself back in Tingle Reef."

"Tingle Reef sounds a wonderful place," Peri said. "And you're so lucky having a mother and a father."

Rani agreed that she *was* lucky. "But the Mer-King and Queen are so kind," she said. "So *you're* lucky too!"

That night, the Mer-King and his wife were throwing a royal banquet in honour of their granddaughter and everyone was invited.

"You'll get to meet all my friends," Peri said, as he began to list them.

Rani started to think about all her friends in Tingle Reef. How was Roscoe getting on without her? And Octavius? And when she thought about Kai she got a funny little ache right in her middle, as if a part of her was missing.

That evening as everyone gathered in the palace, Morva was looking especially beautiful in a multi-coloured top with gold tassels. Her hair seemed even shinier than it had done in Tingle Reef. Rani could see that she was very happy to be back home again.

"Don't you miss your lobsters and your starfish?" she whispered, as she waited in line beside Morva, shaking hands with all the guests as they arrived.

"A little, but, oh . . . Rani . . . I can't help wishing that I'd come back years ago!"

"But then I would never have discovered who I really was," Rani reminded her. "And you wouldn't have been able to teach me all that magic!"

"That's true," Morva smiled. "But I've been thinking, Rani – you don't need me to teach you any more."

"Yes, I do!" protested Rani.

"No, you don't. You are strong enough to manage by yourself from now on. And that's why . . . I've decided to stay here."

"What?" Rani gasped. "But you promised Mother and Father you'd take me back!"

"I promised them I'd get you back *safely* – and I will. But, Rani, this is my true home – not Tingle Reef. I don't have any family to go back to. And after all, I can always go back and visit."

"You can do that too, Rani," the Mer-King added, overhearing them. "You can go back and visit your friends in Tingle Reef whenever you like."

"Oh, but I shan't need to *visit* them," Rani said, feeling confused. "I'll be going back there to stay."

"But you have found your real home now – and your real family," the Mer-King said. "Doesn't that make a difference?"

"My *real* home is in Tingle Reef," Rani protested. "And Mother and Father and Kai and Pearl *are* my real family!"

The Mer-King frowned and it was clear that he didn't agree.

"I have an idea," said Morva thoughtfully. "The message-stone will always show a magic mermaid her true family when she is separated from them. If, in your heart, you believe that your family in Tingle Reef is your true family, Rani . . ." – she pointed to Rani's pendant – "Well, why don't you look inside and see?"

Rani lifted up her pendant. She hadn't even opened the stone since she had met Peri.

As Rani blew on the stone and saw its hard shiny surface turn soft and watery, she started to smile.

"Are they there?" asked Morva.

Rani nodded. And as she gazed happily at the four familiar faces, she knew that it was time for her to go back to them.

"I'll come back and visit you, I promise," Rani said to Peri, who was upset when she told him her plans. Then she had a better idea. "I know! Why don't you come back with me and visit Tingle Reef?"

Peri asked the Mer-King, who thought it was a splendid idea.

"I shall send you both back in my special carriage. You will be quite safe because my dolphins will take care of you!"

And so it was settled. The only thing left to do was say goodbye to Morva.

"I'll really miss you," Rani said,

hugging her friend, as they waited for the royal carriage to arrive. "Are you sure you won't come with us? What about your floating cave? And what will I tell Octavius?"

"My floating cave can be my holiday home," Morva said brightly. "I intend to come back and visit you all soon – you can tell Octavius that!"

"Thank you for everything, Morva," Rani said. "I don't know what I'd have done if you hadn't been there to help me."

"Well, you might not have discovered all this . . ." Morva admitted. "But tell me, Rani, now that you *have* found it, won't it make you *unhappy* having to give it up?"

"I won't be giving it up," Rani told her, smiling. "I'll be coming back again one day. And anyway – it's all in here!" And she tapped her head to show Morva that everything she had found here was stored safely inside.

Chapter Eight

"It's *Rani*!" shouted Kai, as she spotted her sister swimming towards their cave. "Rani – I've missed you so much!"

Their mother appeared, her long blonde hair swirling around her. "My darling!" she cried, rushing to greet her daughter.

"I'm so glad to be home, Mother!" Rani said, as they hugged.

Murdoch swam out of the cave with Pearl and shouted in delight as he saw his daughter again.

"You must come inside and tell us everything," Miriam said, taking her hand. "Where is Morva?"

"I've got so much to tell you," Rani gasped. "But first I want you to come with me. There's someone I'd like you to meet. You see . . . I found my brother. His name's Peri. I wanted to come and see you myself first, so I've left him with Octavius."

They all swam together to Octavius's cave.

"*Wow!*" exclaimed Kai, unable to believe her eyes. The royal carriage was parked outside and the dolphins were out of their harnesses, tucking into large helpings of Octavius's stew.

Inside the octopus's cave, they found Octavius telling Peri that he had guessed all along that Rani was a princess.

"A *princess*?" Kai said, gaping at her sister.

"It's a long story," Rani said, blushing.

"I think you'd better tell it to us right away," said Murdoch.

They all sat and listened as Rani and

Peri explained how they had been separated as babies long ago and that, while Rani was growing up in Tingle Reef, Peri had been brought up by their grandparents, the Mer-King and Queen.

"The Mer-King and Queen?" gasped Kai. "You mean . . . you mean, Rani really is a *princess*?"

Rani and Peri nodded.

Kai had non-stop questions for them after that – and so did everybody else. And they all wanted to see how the message-stone worked.

Rani let out a startled gasp as she opened the stone.

"What's wrong?" everyone asked.

"Nothing," Rani said, frowning. "It's just that *Morva* is inside." She looked at

Peri. "And s*he's* not family."

"I guess you must *think* of her like she is," her brother explained. "A message-stone can always pick up on these things!"

Rani thought about that for a moment. It was true that she had always *felt* very close to Morva. She started to smile as she looked into the stone again.

"Now I'll always be able to see her, even though she's not with me," Rani said happily.

"That's wonderful, darling!" her mother said, reaching out and stroking Rani's hair. "Now, children . . . I know this is all very exciting but it really is time for bed. You must be very tired – *especially* Rani and Peri!"

"Mother is a bit bossy, but you'll get used to her," Rani whispered to her brother.

"I think she's great!" Peri whispered back. "So is your father – *and* your sisters! You're so lucky to have *two* families!"

Rani just smiled. But she had a feeling that by the time Peri left Tingle Reef, *he* was going to have an extra family too.